THE LAST GAMBIT

Om Swami is a mystic who lives in the Himalayan foothills. Prior to renunciation, he founded and ran a multi-million dollar software company with offices across the world. He is also the author of six bestselling books including *If Truth be Told: A Monk's Memoir, The Wellness Sense, When All Is Not Well* and *Kundalini: An Untold Story.*

His blog on spirituality, www.omswami.com, is read by millions all over the world.

THE LAST GAMBIT

OM SWAMI

Published in India by HarperCollins Publishers India Ltd.

Worldwide publishing rights: Black Lotus Press

Copyright © Om Swami 2017

P-ISBN: 978-93-5264-092-8
E-ISBN: 978-93-5264-093-5

Om Swami asserts the moral right to be identified
as the author of this work.

www.omswami.com

In a country where cricket is a religion, this book is dedicated to the unsung heroes of our nation who have brought us glory by silently playing chess with the Indian flag on their desks. Their quiet personalities cloak thousands of hours of practice – and often hardships – like embers mask fire.

When they win world championships and prestigious contests, we don't run out on to the streets bursting crackers. Hundreds of shutterbugs don't go into a tizzy trying to capture them in action. These geniuses don't trend on Twitter, there is no grand public reception or fanfare in their honour. Instead, they get down at the airport, collect their own luggage, go home unnoticed and practise more chess.

This book is a salute to these brilliant minds of our nation.

THE MAGIC PILL

I DON'T KNOW why, but it's really irritating when people get all philosophical and tell me that life is like chess. Yeah, right. How can you even compare the two? For one thing, chess has rules. It is an elegant work of art, whereas life, life is a freaking hammer. Even if it falls elegantly, it crushes you.

In chess, you know exactly when the flag is going down. You can get extra time. You can play games and outmanoeuvre your opponent. But life sees through your tricks. It just comes and slaps you out of your illusions. There is no warning, no indication. Forget extra time.

The year was 1983 and I had just turned fourteen. Not sure if you think it's important, but India had also won its first ever cricket World Cup – a fact not relevant to me any more than the size of a dinosaur's egg.

'*Paidal chalao*, move your foot soldier,' he remarked.

We burst out laughing, for he had called a pawn a foot soldier. What kind of person calls a pawn a foot-soldier? Was this crude old man really playing in our tournament or was he just a spectator? We squeezed some more laughs out of his lingo and the way he was dressed: plain and uncle-ji like.

He showed no reaction though. The bulging eyes behind his big glasses were fixed on the chessboard. This was a casual game among two amateurs during the break of an open chess tournament, open to players of all ages. I couldn't be sure if he was playing the tournament though for, right now, he was simply a spectator like the rest of us.

Each time the old goose   who looked as out of place in our tournament as a faded chess piece among shiny new ones – referred to any piece in Hindi, we guffawed. Some of us even provoked him to speak, to suggest a move. But he remained annoyingly indifferent to our laughter and comments.

The first thing that came to my mind when I saw his face was chai-patti. After they had been boiled and sieved, that is. Maybe a bit darker, actually. He was tall and slim, and wore a hand-knit woollen jumper which was a little faded and looked every bit as old as him.

The bell rang for the fourth round. It was a round-robin tournament of eleven games, of which I had won the previous two out of three games.

I opened the fourth game carefully. Twenty moves later, my position was pretty solid and I was one pawn up. I launched the offence with confidence, but my plan backfired when my opponent planted his knight in a U-pawn chain in the centre. Fifteen moves later, I had nothing to boast about my position. With two pawns down, bishops exchanged and other pieces on the defence, he had ramrodded me out of a good game with his clever play and sheer patience.

While I calculated at lightning speed, he would just sit there and think and think and think, like Rodin's 'Thinker'. I didn't know if I was exasperated because I didn't have his patience or he my speed. Either way, due to minor errors, a perfectly fine game slipped out of my hand.

Just then, the old man appeared on the scene and stood there, observing my game like my grandmother watching her poppadoms frying in the pan. Tournament rules allowed strangers to observe, provided they didn't talk to or prompt players in any way. Though he didn't speak, the old man's silent presence ushered in a wave of embarrassment. Nothing on the chessboard was in my favour.

My opponent had been staring at the board for the last ten minutes.

If he makes any mistake, O Hanuman, I'll go to your temple on Tuesday and offer you modaks. I'll even feed the monkeys in the zoo. Anything to win your favour, I prayed silently.

I prayed that my opponent miscalculates so I could walk away with a point. But Hanuman did not hear me.

My opponent failed to capitalize too. The game wore on for a little while and then went for a draw. We shook hands. I slammed my chess set shut and stuffed the wooden losers in my flabby bag.

Scoring half a point each, we approached the bench to report the result.

'You should have won,' the old fella said, walking up behind me.

'Yeah, I know.' *I don't think I asked for your advice.*

'Then why didn't you?'

'Excuse me?' I said curtly.

'Yes, I'm asking,' he said gravely, 'if you knew then why *didn't* you win?'

His emphasis on *didn't* ticked me off.

'It's none of your business,' I said, and briskly walked the other way.

'It is yours, though,' he hollered from behind.

How I wanted to turn around and sock him with my board for rubbing it in. I took a few steps, but something within – to date I don't know what – made me turn around. He was still standing there, with a mocking smile that made me angrier. At one level I wished that he would disappear, but somewhere, deep down, I was grateful for his presence.

'Tame your impatience if you are serious about winning,' he said.

I wanted to shout at him, call him names, but instead replied, 'Sorry, I didn't mean to be rude.' Maybe because he was showing me the mirror, or maybe because I couldn't make up my mind about his being sincere or sarcastic.

'I know I had a strong attack with the bishops.' I moved closer.

'What bishops? They were resting on the table when I saw you,' he said blandly. 'I'm talking about the rook-and-knight attack.'

'Yeah, right. He had his queen staring at my rook. I'm just lucky I could even draw.'

'Listen up, kiddo.' His knobbly fingers held my thin wrist and he dragged me to a nearby table. There was conviction, a firmness to his grip; no force.

Right in front of my eyes, he reconstructed the exact board position I had when he had emerged on the scene. I was taken aback – I can reconstruct a game all right but no way could I have gone so far back as he had.

'Here, Qg8+ Rg8, Nf7++. There's your check and mate in two moves. All forced moves. He was trapped behind his own pawns.'

I stared.

His hands had moved with remarkable speed on the board, as if he was collecting his poker winnings and not playing chess. There was no clumsiness, no holes – this was a foolproof attack.

I hate to admit it, but I was humbled. He no longer looked shabby to me. What I saw now was the intelligence which shone on his face, bright and clear.

'Tell me if he had any choice at all? And you think that was the only attack you had?'

I hadn't yet got over the first attack he'd coined, and here he was going on about another one. I thought it best to keep quiet rather than cement my position as a clueless ass.

'Pay attention now.' He quickly moved pieces to draw the original position on the board, pushed two pawns and drew a knight fork, forcing the opponent to give up his queen for a measly knight. 'You could have had his queen, and two passed pawns.'

Passed pawns are prized possessions in the end game; they are two pawns, one protecting the other; the opponent captures the one at the back and the one in front starts moving to the end of the board where it can become a queen, bishop, rook or a knight. If unchecked, pawn promotion in the case of passed pawns is nearly unavoidable.

'How do I improve my game?' I blurted.

'Why do you play chess?'

'I like this game!'

'You play because you *like* it?' There it was again – the mocking tone. 'You think it's *just a game*?' He shook his head, and mumbled, 'Huh, game…'

I liked chess all right, and I practised hard, but I didn't think it was any more than a game, a pastime, albeit a damn good one. Besides, what more could it be anyway? It's not like I was a chess prodigy, born into a family of chess champions, slowly inching my way to the top. No one in my family even knew how to play the game. My mother thought I needed to eat more almonds because chess was using up my brain, and my father only supported me because he thought it was better than spending my time running around with the good-for-nothing kids on our street. My sister, Mira, didn't know how to play, and my brother, Varun, couldn't care less. If anything, Varun teased me about chess, calling me Munshiji after Munshi Premchand's *Shatranj ke Khiladi*.

There was no one to coach me for miles. There were no grandmasters in my town. Heck, there were only five in the whole country. And even if there were, we could not afford coaching, for I belonged to a simple middle-class family, the type that wore hand-knit sweaters and not readymade ones. We were not the carriers of civilization but the bearers of mediocrity because our outfits had no logos. No Nike, Adidas or Monte Carlo.

Coaching was for the rich. Mostly. Plus, there was a reason why I was more arrogant than confident: I believed I wasn't champion material.

As if reading my mind, he said, 'Champions are not born, Vasu. They are made. And no one really makes them. Champions make themselves.'

'How do you know my name?' I asked, startled.

'Duh! I read it on the pairing sheet outside.'

'You think I can be a champion?'

'Do *you* think you can be one?'

'If I have you, then yes.'

'Why me?'

I didn't know what to say. As soon as I said it, I knew it to be true. It was as if my heart had a mind of its own, and was doing its own thinking, and had already made its decision.

'My heart says so.'

The bell echoed through the corridors. It was time for the next round. But I didn't turn away. Standing in his presence was melting something in me. As if, already, he was silently teaching me, transforming me.

'Will you coach me, please?' I got up, went to his side of the table and reached out to touch his feet. It felt right.

He didn't pull me up. Or stop me. But he was quiet, his eyes a little moist. I'm not sure if that was because of his age or if he was feeling sentimental.

'On two conditions,' he said.

'Conditions?'

'Yes. First, you will never dig into my past. Second, I'll never accompany you to any tournaments.'

'Whatever you say.'

'Listen, son,' he said after a brief pause. 'There is no magic pill. Whatever you want in life, you have to earn it. And remember, chess is not a game, it's a way of life.'

'I'll do anything to learn from you.'

'Anything?'

'I swear by Bajrang Bali.'

A faint smile appeared on his face. 'If chess is the only thing you want in life and if you promise to not leave it in between,' he spoke solemnly, 'I'll make you a grandmaster.'

Grandmaster. My heart skipped a beat. A surge of energy passed through me. I wanted to jump in the air and touch the sky. I wanted to hug him.

'Sleep over it. Speak to your parents. And if you are ready, I will see you here tomorrow.'

He got up and walked away with swift, steady steps. His head was lowered, and I got the feeling that he saw the floor like a chessboard.

Rocking my world, he had left me with a dream.

Of everything he'd said, one statement kept bouncing against the walls of my mind – champions make themselves. I ran to the pairing sheet since I was already late for my game. Though I went on to win the remaining two games that day, I was distracted. More than winning the tournament, I craved to play with him, to learn from him. His words had set the bird in my chest free. I felt like a caterpillar crawling out of my cocoon to become a butterfly.

I rode back home in the evening on my girlie ride, my moped. Other kids at school often made fun of me. It bothered me sometimes, but never enough to abandon it. I knew that was all my parents could afford. Today, I didn't notice the shops, food stalls, people, traffic, nothing. Lost in my own world, I was home before I knew it.

My father, a government employee, a serious man, was reading a newspaper while Mira and Varun, my elder siblings, were sitting nearby, studying. Father always handed his entire salary to my mother, a homemaker and a very wise woman who managed the finances carefully.

'Oh, Vasu's home!' Mother came rushing out of the kitchen. She cupped my face with her hands; they were warm. I was already a little taller than her. Although she would never admit it in front of my siblings, in private she would tell me that I was her favourite.

'Can I ask you a question, dad?'

'Hmm,' he said, not looking up from the newspaper.

'It's serious, dad.'

He lowered the newspaper.

'I'll be back in a moment. Milk is on the stove.' Mom went to the kitchen, turned off the stove, and returned in a flash.

'What if I direct all my focus on to chess ... to become a grandmaster?'

'What do you mean by *all* your focus?'

'I mean, I will study, but what if I make chess my priority?'

His face turned serious. 'Chess is good, son, but it is not going to pay your bills. There—'

'But it's my dream, dad,' I said impatiently.

'Since when? And life doesn't run on dreams, Vasu,' he said firmly. 'Chess is not a career option.'

It's not that I disagreed with him. The popular career paths, doctor, engineer, accountant, etc., were safe choices. But I couldn't get the old man out of my head, neither the word 'grandmaster' that he had so casually dropped.

'Studies are important, Vasu,' mom chipped in.

'I'm not saying I won't study,' I said angrily. I needed her by my side. 'It's just that I will pursue a less demanding course. Chess is where my heart is. I want to become a grandmaster.'

'But Vasu, beta—'

'Do you even know the price of a litre of milk?' dad asked, cutting mom off.

'I let you play chess so you get a break from your studies,' he continued. 'You guys get everything easy and that's why you don't know the value of anything. You think life is all rosy?'

Oh no, not another lecture!

He kept that up for another ten minutes, none of which I tuned into, except some sentences here and there. He said something about chess not giving me a livelihood, and that everything was so expensive these days. I think he also brought up how my mother's softness was doing all the damage. At first I was angry because I knew he would have the last word. But as he kept lecturing, I felt alienated and lonely.

Some more time passed and he was still going on about how hard he had to work in life, and that I had no clue how competitive the world out there was. I felt helpless. I tried to act strong, but I couldn't stop my eyes from welling up.

At this, dad paused for a few seconds and then started again. Finally, mom put a hand on his shoulder and pleaded with him to stop. She wasn't going to pacify me in front of my father, especially when he was the one scolding me. We all knew strongly he disapproved of such gestures.

By now, tears were rolling down my eyes, but no one got up to make me feel better. I think my crying melted his heart, but not enough for him to grant me my wish. The middle-class could not afford such luxuries.

'You are only fourteen, Vasu, and you don't know what's right for you. This new fascination of yours will disappear in a few days,' he said, dismissing me. 'Go, have dinner now.'

He went back to his newspaper. I stormed into the room I shared with my brother. When mom came in a little later, I did not want to talk to her. She had betrayed me by not supporting me at all. When she asked me to come for dinner, I retorted I was not hungry and sent her away.

You are useless, Bajrang Bali, I said to the little statue of Hanuman sitting on my side table. *You can't make anything happen. Ever. I'm never talking to you again.*

As always, he was smiling at me, the mace effortlessly sitting on his shoulder. I turned him to face the wall. *Look the other way.*

A couple of hours went by. Varun came into our room. He was four years elder to me and cracked jokes to make me laugh. He failed. Mira, six years elder to me, tried to console me by saying that dad would eventually grant me permission, but she was just trying to make me feel better. Mother only seemed concerned about my dinner right then, but I was adamant.

There was a knock on the door, followed by absolute silence. My face was buried in the pillow, but because of the sudden silence, I knew dad had just entered the room.

'Vasu?' He came near me, dragged the chair next to my study table and sat on it.

I did not respond.

'Vasu? Beta? Listen to me,' he said in his deep voice.

I raised my head and sat up. Mira and Varun sat on Varun's bed, and my mother took the chair from his study table.

'You know that your mother and I are your greatest well-wishers, right? We are only thinking about your welfare?'

I nodded.

'What happened today at the tournament? You came home and suddenly wanted to pursue chess instead of studies?'

'What's the point telling you?' I growled. 'It's not like you'll say, "okay, go play chess".'

'At least *tell* me, Vasu.'

I narrated the story of the old man to my parents. 'He said he would teach me if and only if chess is my sole priority.'

'Is this what you really want to do? Do you want to reconsider?' He sounded much gentler now.

'I thought about it all day. This is the only thing I want to do.'

'I am only worried because it is your future we are talking about.'

'Have faith, dad,' I said confidently. 'I won't disappoint you.'

'It's not going to be a piece of cake, you know.' He ran his hand through my hair. Everyone smiled, because we knew that whenever he gave in, rather than saying 'yes', he made a loving gesture.

'How much will he charge?' I could see a trace of concern in his calm eyes. But the question meant that he had nearly agreed.

I got up and rammed into him. 'Oh, I love you so much, daddy.'

'Okay, okay,' he said. 'What's his fee?'

'I didn't ask him.'

'I would like to meet him once,' he said, and left the room.

'What's this?' Varun said to mum. 'When *I* wanted to play cricket, I was told to shut up and focus on my studies! But in just a few hours, Vasu gets permission to play chess? This is not fair,' he protested. 'I want a new bike.'

'Good try.' Mother smiled and walked out.

'You know you are not getting a new bike,' I teased my brother.

'Fine, then. You win some big prize money, Kasparov Bhatt, and buy me a bike,' he said mockingly.

I picked up a pillow to throw it at him but he had already dashed out.

'And next time, don't cry like a little girl. Boo hoo,' he called back.

I tried to play some practice games in preparation of the tournament the next day, but just couldn't focus. I tried to sleep after dinner, but couldn't do that either. I kept tossing and turning. A million questions were bothering me. What if my teacher asked for too much money? What if I never became a grandmaster? I looked up at the clock: already an hour past midnight. I was feeling tired and my eyes were a little heavy. The train of my thoughts shifted and I started dreaming about winning tournaments, titles, prize money...

The alarm woke me up. I had a hurried breakfast and rushed out for the second day at the tournament. I couldn't wait to see him, my dream maker.

2

ON BOARD, OFF BOARD

THE PARKING STAND was nearly full by the time I got to the venue. Some of the older players – many with grey hair – were already practising, having set up their chessboards on their bikes. The ones who smoked preferred to practise in the parking lot, puffing away at their cigarettes. I rushed inside to speak to the old man, my master.

I saw a few familiar faces from the previous day; more players were trickling in. The officials were walking around, checking the arrangements. In the corridors, on the benches, players were playing casual games while onlookers watched and commented. Some were analysing their games from the previous day, some just sipping tea and eating bread pakoras.

I couldn't find the only person I was looking for. Like a calf separated from its mother, before I even checked the lists that day, I went around searching for the old man. I ran to every group to see if he was there. I even inspected the washrooms. He was nowhere. The day had just begun; so, though I was anxious, I didn't think much of it. I was trying to be patient, I had no other choice anyway. Maybe he will come a bit later, I thought.

My ranking looked good at start of the day; I was in second place with four-and-a-half points. The player in front was only half a point ahead. The competition was getting tougher too, since winners were playing winners. I was playing black in my next game, which meant my opponent would open with white.

I made every move as if my life depended on it. The caution and calculation paid off and I won the game without any major upsets. I was suddenly on the top of the chart. It was a good feeling but with four more games to go and no sign of the old man, I was beginning to feel uneasy and distracted. Once again, I barged into every group, and checked the washrooms. I looked in the office. I ran into every person I didn't give a damn about. Just not him.

Dismayed, I couldn't focus on the next two games. I gave a tough fight but lost both due to minor but expensive mistakes. I was at number five on the chart now. It was no longer the chart but the absence of the old man that worried me. He was nowhere, and I didn't even have his contact details. This tournament was not at a regular chess club; it was a high school turned into a tournament venue for the weekend. If I missed him that day, I would have no way of reaching him.

The second-last game drew and, with my score of six out of ten, I had gone from topping to being sixth on the chart. I was playing the last game under tremendous stress. The whole day had passed and the old man was still not here.

'Vasu Bhatt?' The referee approached me in the middle of my game.

'Yes?'

'There's someone here to see you. It's urgent, he says.'

'Oh, thank you!' I got up and threw my hands up in the air. 'Yes, it is very urgent.'

I didn't ask where. I just ran to the door. That's one thing I've always liked about chess, unlike any other game, you can just get up and leave while the clock is still ticking.

But I didn't find the old man waiting for me. The referee too was out by now.

'He's waiting just outside the main office.'

'Thank you so much!' I flew like a poorly tied shoe off a flopping foot.

He was not there either.

'Bhaiya ji?' A familiar voice called out to me.

'Mewa?' It was our maid's husband. *Him? I ran for him? What was he doing here?* He was standing there calmly, and I felt like banging my head against the wall.

'You forgot your tiffin at home,' he said. 'Your mum has been worried sick since morning. She said it was way past your lunch time.'

'Mum!' I ground my teeth.

'Varun bhaiya is out playing cricket and your father has taken Mira didi to a painting exhibition,' he continued solemnly. 'I was specially called back from home to bring you this tiffin. I came here as fast as I could.'

'Take it back,' I shouted. 'I'm not hungry.'

He placed the tiffin between the bars of a window and walked away.

'Sorry, Mewa,' I said, holding him by the wrist. 'I didn't mean to yell.'

'It's okay.' He gently released himself from my grip and went his way.

I picked up my tiffin and went back to my game, feeling bad about my behaviour, equally frustrated with the world, mad at mum, and madder at the old man.

The clock was ticking. I had lost five minutes, but my position in the game was strong. I took a few deep breaths to calm myself down and focus again. It was a close-ended, tough fight. In close-ended games, the play is lot more tactical. The two players focus more on building their defences and a longer-term strategy than quickly exchanging pieces to open up the board. I wanted to clear the board, but my opponent stuck to his plan and kept all pieces in play. It was as if he knew I was running low on patience.

What does the old man think? I can't win without him? Revolt has a strange way of giving you strength. It gives you the energy and conviction to stand up for yourself. Even if foolishly and temporarily, it makes you fearless. Right then, I was so mad that I could have taken on anyone. I wanted to crush my opponent and that's exactly what I did.

After a close middle game and a tense, long and tiring end game, I won. A couple of mistakes in two earlier games had thrown me from first to fifth and pulled me down real fast. My ranking was the least of my concerns, though. I was only thinking about the old man and felt increasingly angry and helpless at his betrayal.

I wasn't keen on attending the prize distribution ceremony. I didn't want to go on stage to receive a certificate of attendance and a consolation prize of fifty rupees.

But fifty rupees would cover my tournament fee and my fuel expense. So I parked my ego and disappointment aside and attended the ceremony. The emptiness and anxiety of not finding the old man returned soon after. I thought of every possibility for his not showing up, including him dying, meeting with an accident, or forgetting about it, but nothing pacified me. My head was beginning to hurt.

Gradually, the players began to leave the venue. The tournament organizers were wrapping up, the watchman was locking every room. The venue was beginning to look sparse. Players were chatting, discussing their games, analysing where they went wrong. Some were moving towards the front door, many towards the parking stand. I sat there in a chair, in a lonely corner. Where the hell was the old man?

It was already six. It was the month of October, and the sun would disappear by seven. I had to be home before dark; this was the non-negotiable rule.

The watchman asked me to vacate the chair so he could put it back in the room and told me to go home or to the parking stand which had a separate entrance. Casually, I asked him if he knew anything about the old man who attended the previous day. He replied in the negative without even asking me what he looked like.

That's why he's just a petty watchman. Because he's lazy. He'll retire and die as a frigging watchman. I was angry.

I wanted to step on cockroaches, to pluck the legs of a spider and let it crawl on the ground. I wanted to turn a beetle on its back and see it shake its legs in the air helplessly. I felt like feeding a mouse to a cat and watch it maul its meal first.

And then I felt intense sadness engulf me like rainclouds gather in the sky.

I got up and walked towards my moped slowly. What would I say to my parents? I kicked a stone as I got closer to the mostly deserted parking stand.

Someone was sitting on the kerb. His back was towards me but I felt a pull. My heart pounded, it raced. This man's jumper was hand-knit too, and he was slender … could it be him? My pace increased.

There he was, eating a sandwich, the sides of which were sliced. His large glasses looked like they were dancing on his ears as he unhurriedly nibbled on his sandwich. Next to him was a bottle of Campa Cola. I wanted to snatch his sandwich and cola and hurl them at the wall. I felt like shaking him and asking him how come he did not understand the importance of his own words. I wanted to shout at him.

I did none of those things.

'Sit,' he said.

I did not. I was fried.

'I've got a sandwich for you.'

He offered me one. I didn't know him long or well enough to express my anger outright. I sat down.

I was so relieved to see him that a tear rolled down my eyes. Quietly, he brought the sandwich in front of me, a few inches below my nose.

I let a few moments tick before I took it. A faint smile made its way to the edge of my lips.

'I love cola,' he said, 'I play much better when I am drinking cola. What about you, what's your favourite?'

'I looked for you everywhere today,' I said.

'Everywhere?'

'You promised yesterday that you would see me today,' I said, without answering his question.

'It's still today, isn't it?'

'Do you even know how distressed I was?' I complained. 'I got so distracted, I lost my games.'

'Rule number one: focus,' he replied. 'Never let anything distract you. Ever.'

'But, why didn't you show up earlier? I searched for you in every nook and corner.'

'How did you fare?' He didn't seem interested in answering my questions.

'I came fifth.'

'Not bad.'

'Had you showed up in the morning, I would have won all games.'

'You are like the puppy that gets distracted at the sight of a biscuit. A true grandmaster never lets anything distract him. Ever. It could be your mother's dead body lying next to you but you must play your game calmly.'

'I searched for you everywhere!'

'Clearly, you didn't look in the parking lot. Did you? I was here the whole day.' Then he said, 'Eat your sandwich.' And he pulled out a chilled bottle of cola from a bag that looked insulated. 'Here, have this.'

I rested the sandwich in my lap and opened the bottle. Tsss ... Oh, that sound! Now I was both hungry and thirsty. I devoured it and quickly gulped down the cola.

'No matter how lucrative it appears, no matter how hungry you are, never rush. Like the sandwich and the drink, it's all in front of you, yours for the taking, but rushing is erring,' he said. 'Another sandwich?'

I could do with another one, but I was feeling shy. I just looked at him quietly. Behind his glasses, his eyes no longer looked bulgy or funny.

He pulled out another sandwich. I took it and unwrapped it quickly, but finished it slowly. He thrust another cola in my hands.

He continued, 'You see, whenever you win because of a carefully executed strategy, you always feel full, like you did after the second sandwich. If you win because your opponent made a grave mistake or you got lucky, then win you may, but you won't feel as if you've earned it. Always go for the complete meal, you know what I mean?'

I nodded. I still hadn't got over the fact that I'd found someone like him.

'Your parents must be waiting for you.'

'Oh, can I please talk to you about a couple of important things?'

'Hmm.'

'I spoke to my parents—'

'I know they agreed. That's why I spent the last half hour teaching you.'

'Yes, they did, but my father was asking about the fees. He also wants to meet you.'

'He's a good father.' He took a sip from his bottle. 'I will talk to him. How about now?'

'Now?'

'Sure, why not?'

My heart pounded. What if the old man charged more than we could afford? It was a good idea to clear it up as soon as possible. I could not wait to get started either.

'So, will you follow me?'

'I'm on a bicycle. I know the lone moped parked in this lot is yours. You give me the address, I'll reach there by myself.'

His lack of material comforts mattered no more to me. However, I worried whether my father would accept him. He might even argue that if I spent my time just playing chess, my old age would be like my teacher's – impoverished. Another thought crossed my mind: if he was such a great player, how come he could not afford a car or even a scooter? But it was just that – a fleeting thought.

I jotted down my address at the back of a blank scoring sheet.

'If you want, I can ride slowly and we can go together.'

'It's okay, Vasu, you carry on. I'll see you in thirty minutes. You go at your pace and I'll reach at mine. This is something you should know in the game too: never let your opponent alter your pace of play with his moves, tricks or gimmicks. Learn to move at the pace *you* are comfortable with, learn to alter it effortlessly when necessary. You make fewer mistakes that way.'

I touched his feet, a little hastily, for when I got up, he was still placing his hand on my head to bless me, and I ran to my moped.

My moped was not designed to go more than thirty kilometres an hour. It felt particularly slow that day. I parked as fast I could and slam-opened the door. Everyone was in the living room, watching the Sunday evening movie. There was no cable TV back then. Only one channel: Doordarshan. A programme featuring Bollywood songs on Wednesday and a movie every Sunday were just about the only attractions, unless you enjoyed watching classical music and *Krishi Darshan*.

'Mum! Dad!' I shouted.

They were happy to see me gleaming, hyper.

'Looks like someone won the tournament today,' exclaimed my mother. 'He's coming home. My teacher!' I shrieked. 'He'll be here in fifteen minutes. He's coming to talk to you.' I looked at my father.

'*Now?* Is he coming *now?*' mom interjected. 'Oh my God, what am I going to feed him? Go quickly, run to the shop and get some sweets and samosas. It is dinner time. Also get some yogurt. He might have his dinner here. Do you know what he likes to eat?' We knew her instructions were for my elder brother but her question was for me.

My mother would never let anyone leave our home unfed. How could I know what he liked? I only saw him eating sandwiches. 'Oh yes, get a Campa for him,' I said. 'He likes cola.'

She forgot all about the movie, rushed to the kitchen and called Mira to help her. Varun was already taking cash out of dad's wallet to get the things mom had mentioned. Each time he got a chance to buy anything from the shops, he would use the opportunity to buy something for himself as well: a pen, potato chips, chewing gum, some junk item, basically. It was at the most once or twice a month that we bought such things from the shops, or if someone visited our home at a short notice, like that day.

The volume of the television suddenly went up – it was a commercial break. This was a black-and-white TV with no mute button or even a remote. Dad quickly got up and turned the volume down.

'Did he tell you about the fee?'

'He said he would talk to you directly about it.'

'Turn on the light outside. It'll be easier for him to read the house number.' We were always careful about turning off lights. 'Every rupee counts,' my father would say often.

'And how was the tournament?'

'Oh, I came fifth.'

He smiled. 'That's good. I'm proud of you.' Dad never burdened anyone with his expectations.

I went to the kitchen and returned the tiffin box to my mother. She looked aghast, appalled, for it felt heavy to her. 'You did not eat your lunch today? Oh my God, what do I do with this boy?'

'Mum, I—'

'What mum?' she cut in. 'It took us two hours to trace Mewa Singh and I practically pleaded with him to deliver your tiffin.'

'Relax, mum. Relax. Sir gave me sandwiches and I had cola.'

'That junk is not filling. You are a growing boy, you need proper nutrition.'

I planted a kiss on her cheek, brushed aside her concern with a laugh and went to my room to put my chess set back. I then took off my shoes and slipped into something comfy. I was still young enough to cuddle and kiss my mother then. It made me stronger, it made me softer.

There was a knock on the door. We did not have a doorbell – the good ones cost over a hundred rupees. Dad spent both his time and his money with utmost care.

I ran to the door, barefoot. I wanted to be the first one at the door to welcome him.

'Hahaha…' Varun said. It was bloody Varun playing a prank. He laughed his head off, and I was quite annoyed.

'Hot samosas, cold rasgullas, chilled cola! Yum yum!' he said, trying to lure and tease me at the same time.

'Huh!' I went back to my room and he to the kitchen. While setting the plates, he would always eat one or two. Always. And he was the first to leap towards the plates as soon as the guests left. He had pledged to never leave anything for the next day, except his homework, of course.

I was barely back in my room when someone knocked again. This was a softer knock. I ran out once again, with my slippers on this time. It was him. My father came to the door as well.

'Namaste,' he said with folded hands greeting our elderly guest.

'Namaste.' My teacher looked back at his bicycle, wondering if it was okay to leave it outside.

'Oh, I'll get your bicycle, sir,' I said, and ran out to park the old but immaculately clean bicycle.

Meanwhile, Dad led him in.

My teacher was seated in the drawing room, which was the most well-decorated, well-kept room in the house. We were not allowed to play there or entertain our friends in that room; it was reserved for the more important guests.

My brother entered first, with the plates of food. He touched my teacher's feet and sat on the couch closest to the plates. My sister came next.

'Namaste.' She was holding a plate of pakoras.

'God bless you,' he replied.

My mother came in last with glasses of cola on a tray.

'Namaste,' she said, placing the tray on the centre table.

'God bless you, beti.'

Dad placed a glass of the cold drink in front of him. I shivered a little thanks to my nervousness.

'Thank you, but I'm sorry,' my teacher said. 'I don't drink cola after sunset. It doesn't let me sleep.'

'Would you like tea?'

'No, thank you.'

'Coffee?'

'No, I'm okay. Thanks.'

'Have some milk, then,' mom offered. Her guest must drink something!

'Okay, I'll have some milk.'

'Do you take sugar?'

'One spoon.'

She returned to the kitchen.

Varun was grinning, probably visualizing himself with the bottle of cola.

Dad struck up a conversation about the weather, about the state of our nation and other irrelevant things. He was waiting for my master to initiate the main topic.

Mom came back with the milk and placed it in front of our guest.

In between sips of milk and the rasgullas, samosas and pakoras that were constantly proffered and various off-the-track topics, he came to the point.

'I saw your son play yesterday,' he said. 'He has potential. Enormous potential. Just needs good guidance and a lot of practice.'

I looked at my mother. She was getting emotional. Mira was smiling with a sisterly pride. And Varun, he was looking at the samosas. Unblinkingly.

'Vasu mentioned that you coach,' dad said. 'That you are willing to train him.'

'I don't coach, normally. I haven't taught anyone in the last thirty years, but yes, I'd be happy to train your son.'

'That's very kind of you. By the way, may I please know your name?'

'Anand. Anand Sharma,' he replied, looking directly into my eyes. 'I was a rated chess player once.'

'To be honest with you,' dad said, 'I don't know much about chess, but this is what Vasu wants to pursue.'

He fell quiet. There was a solemn silence in the room, which was rudely broken when Varun banged his hand against a plate while trying to pick up a pakora he had dropped on the floor.

God, how I hated him at that moment.

'We were wondering if you would charge per month or for the full course,' dad said.

My master chuckled.

'I don't want any money. My fee will be his time. Every day, straight after the school, he should be at my home for four hours. During the weekends, I'll need all his time. He can even sleep at my house. I am seventy-seven years old. I live alone and there's a maid who comes for an hour daily and cleans the house and does the dishes. I cook my own food. I don't mind feeding him too. Or maybe he can offer me a hand there. During his school vacations too, he will need to spend all his time with me. It is through intense training alone that he's going to run like a Ferrari.'

'Oh wow!' Varun squealed. 'A Ferrari? That's what they gave Kapil Dev for winning the cricket World Cup!'

I wish I could just burn him with my stare. Besides, they hadn't given him a Ferrari but an Audi.

'Varun!' Father chastised him.

'Listen, kid,' my teacher said to me, 'I'll be giving you all the knowledge I have. All my time. Are you absolutely sure that chess is what you want? Once the boat is undocked, there's no sailing back.'

'I promise.' The voice came all squeaky. I cleared my throat. 'I promise.'

'Are you committed to put in the time as your sir said?'

'Yes, dad.'

'Well then, he's all yours.' Dad smiled at my teacher.

'Let's play to win.' My teacher smiled at me.

'Chess should be the only thing on your mind. When we get tired of analysing, we'll play; when we are tired of playing, we'll analyse; when we are tired of both, we'll watch others play; when we are tired of watching, we'll do chess riddles; when done with riddles, we'll play rapid; when tired of rapid, we'll play blitz; when we want to take a break, we'll play blindfold. The only rest you'll get is either during sleep or while at school. Are you up for it?'

'I'll do whatever you ask me to do,' I said.

He scribbled his contact details on a sheet of paper.

As he got up, everyone touched his feet, for he was almost my dead grandfather's age.

We went outside, all except Varun, who got busy finishing the goodies.

'I didn't say it in there, but not just a grandmaster, I will make you a world champion,' he whispered as I helped him with his bicycle.

I stood there speechless.

We bade him goodbye as he pedalled his way out of our sight but into my heart.

3

A PAPER BOAT

DO YOU THINK I care if the area of the moon is fourteen or fourteen million square miles? This fact is as interesting to me as the dimensions of the red rear of an African baboon. Pushing my boring physics book aside, I dwelled on a novel chess opening, with three lines of attack. Now that's something I would kiss and keep. I had to write it down right away.

'Vasu?' I thought I heard someone call me but I wasn't sure.

'Vasu?'

'Hmm…'

'VASU!' she screamed at me.

'Yes, ma'am,' I said. Thud. 'Oh shoot,' came out as I banged my knee against the desk while standing up. That hurt.

'What were you doing?'

'M … me?' I stammered. 'I was … was making notes about what you were saying.'

'What is the area of moon?'

'Umm … in square kilometres or miles?' I said while rubbing my knee.

She marched straight to my desk, army style. This was the science period at school. Only the third period of the day.

'Show me your notebook,' she demanded.

I didn't utter a word. She picked it up from the desk and glanced at it.

'What's this, e4, e6, g3, b6, f4, Bb7, d4...?'

Now I was genuinely confused. I didn't know if she was actually asking what opening this was, or what I had written.

'I just coined a variation to the standard e4,' I answered seriously.

'What e4!'

Before I could say anything, she shouted, 'Get out of my class!'

'I'm sorry, ma'am,' I mumbled and lowered my head.

'Get out and stay out!'

I looked at my watch. Still thirty minutes to go in the period. It was a bit humiliating but what made it particularly painful was that I wasn't allowed to carry my notebook outside. I had to record any variations in my head now. I walked out of the class and stood there, distressed, for the first few minutes. But then I had an amazing response to the queen's gambit. The day seemed to be one of epiphanies. The next thirty minutes passed in a flash while I was still working out lines of defence in my head.

'You disappoint me, Vasu,' my teacher said as she walked out at the end of the class. Reema Claire. Yeah, that was her name. We had nicknamed her Cadbury, after the Cadbury éclair toffee.

I pretended to hang my head in shame, then went back in to the class with a false and cocky smile. It felt good to sit again.

'You were good, man,' a couple of my friends said.

'Kilometres or miles!' another said. 'That was cool!'

I just smiled and got back to finishing my notes. I had to seek my teacher's opinion on my discovery. Not Cadbury's, Mr Sharma's.

I must have looked at my watch at least a hundred times before the last bell rang and I ran to the parking lot as if my back was on fire.

I headed towards the address he had provided. My little moped was any day faster than a bicycle. It was bought for my sister but she didn't like it. My brother wouldn't touch it because it was beneath his tough image to be seen on a 'girly ride'. So, it ended up with me. Fine, not a girl, at least I had a girly ride. It was a loyal mount that, it got me wherever I needed to go. My little town was my world – I had never been outside it on my own. I asked my way around to reach his home.

There was no nameplate, just a house number in white on an old, rectangular metal plaque, painted black. Rust was visible at the two screws, diagonal to each other, that held it against the wall. The other two were missing. The faded nameplate reminded me of his faded jumper. Just below, facing the street, was a window of his house. It was closed. The house was in an old area of the town. Each house was joined to the next; most even shared a common wall. His main door was through a narrow alley, almost like a corridor. I parked my moped on the street next to his house, climbed up the ramp and there I stood, in front of his main door, a gateway to my dream world. Underneath the doorbell, a hand-written slip was stuck. *Doorbell*, it read. I chuckled.

Trrriing. I could hear the bell ring inside his house.

The few seconds I waited felt like eternity.

Trrrriiiinngg. I pressed again.

Some more time went by. Till date, I remain unsure if it was I who was impatient or if he actually did take a long time to come to the door.

Trrrrriiiiinnnnggg. I buzzed once again, a bit longer, but a little hesitatingly this time. While I didn't want to annoy him, I wasn't exactly enjoying standing expectantly like a monk waiting for alms.

I was about to press it the fourth time, with the intention of gluing my finger to the button. The door opened just then. He opened a little bit first to check who was at the door, saw me and opened it fully. He looked majestic to me just then, standing like that at the door. He was wearing a different pair of glasses, with a nice metal frame. I bent down, only just, to touch his feet, more as a custom than out of reverence.

'Come in.'

The walls were painted yellow, the doors were grey. This was an old house. The couch was comfortable and had fluffy cushions.

'Take a seat,' he said.

My eyes popped at the sight of a large bookcase full of chess books. It was touching the ceiling. Now this was certainly more interesting than the coloured butt of a baboon.

He got two bottles of cola from the fridge; one for each. I noticed the floor was cemented and slightly uneven because the centre table felt wobbly as he placed the bottles on it. I was still looking around furtively when he reached out to a nearby box. My gaze settled immediately – like a hungry dog's would at the sight of food.

It was a mini briefcase, he opened it gently, even elegantly. In it lay a chess mat, chess clock and chessmen – all immaculate. Old. Clean. A little worn from use. He spread the mat on the table and asked me whether I wanted white or black. I picked white.

I thought he would ask me how my day went and all that, but not a word.

Okay! No worries. Serious stuff. I didn't ask him either. *I'll play along.* I wanted to get his opinion on my variations. *Maybe another day.*

'Twenty plus five.' He set the clock to give each of us twenty minutes with an additional five minutes if necessary.

I made my first move – the standard king's pawn opening – the one I knew best. This opening allowed for quicker development of my minor chess pieces, bishops and knights.

He responded like a machine too – by the book. The first six moves were the standard ones. From the seventh move, he started playing differently. It was a variation unknown to me. He was already attacking, all his forces directed at f2, g2 and h2, the squares next to my castled king. Before I knew it, I was on the defensive. His play was tactical and his plot ingenious. My king was cornered before I could finish my drink.

'Checkmate,' he announced.

The game was over in eighteen moves. The clock had only ticked 20 per cent of its allotted time. I was a bit embarrassed about losing like that, but I put on a brave face. *It was only your first game for heaven's sake. Plus, do you see how many books he's read on chess?*

'Let's play one more.' He was white this time.

I reset the clock. *You are not running through my fort this time, sir.*

All my plans failed. They fizzled out like the fizz in my cola while he smothered me in under fifteen moves. The clock was only 10 per cent through this time. He made moves at lightning pace.

I was filled with both awe and fear. I was more intimidated than pissed. I tried to compose myself.

'Wow! You played really fast, sir.'

'Yes, but why did you?' he asked. 'Why did you alter your pace, Vasu? You must never change your tempo to match your opponent's. Don't race with a bike if you are on a moped. Frustrate them; make them slow down to your pace.'

'But, I knew from the word go that I had no chance of winning against you.'

'If you want to rely on chance, go play cards.'

'But, you are a much stronger opponent!' I shrieked.

'That doesn't mean you play a lousy game.'

'I didn't!' I was getting irritated. *God, this man is mean.*

'You certainly played much worse than you did at the tournament.'

'I was nervous, all right,' I admitted petulantly. 'I'm sorry, but I was nervous.'

'Nervous?' He threw his head back and laughed. 'Vasu,' he said gravely. 'There's no room, nor reason, for being nervous in chess.'

Something in his voice calmed me down.

'Let me tell you a little story.' He drank more cola, sat back and started talking in a faraway tone. 'I was just about your age, a year younger, maybe.'

'I was from a small village and it was my first tournament in a town. I rode all the way, twenty kilometres on my bicycle. The only bus to the town was never on time and there was no other mode of transportation available. I reached the venue two hours early, spread my chess mat, opened my book and started practising. Other players began trickling in and soon the place was abuzz.

India was still under the British Raj and there were two separate halls for brown and white people. Everyone knew that the hall for the whites had a table set-up with coffee, tea, water and snacks while ours had nothing in it. Their hall was equipped with ceiling fans, desks and chairs whereas our hall had mats spread on the ground. We were to sit on the ground and play, much like how it had been in my village school.

It was a matter of great prestige to play against a white guy. If a brown person made impressive wins, he would be pitted against a white. He was then allowed to play in the hall reserved for whites. In any case, even if we made to the other hall, we were not allowed to partake of their refreshments. In fact, we could be jailed if we made any such attempt.

For a chess player, all of this was okay, even bearable to some degree for this was how things were at the time. What was painful though, was a violation of the spirit of the game. When playing against a white person, we would always get the black pieces. Normally, you get white in every alternate game but not in a tournament where firangis played. They would always get to open with white.

Anyway, starting in the brown hall, I got black in the first game. I knew nothing about my opponent. None of us had a chess clock. I won the first game within minutes of the bell going off. It wasn't a smothered or a fool's mate. I did not win it because he was an idiot. I just managed to find a powerful mating attack. We went to a room where the organizers sat to register our result.

Game number two, I was white, my competition was tougher this time. I opened conventionally and played carefully. I made every move with extreme caution. It was my first big tournament, so I took my games very seriously. 'I won this one too, not as easily as my first game, though.

Game number three, I was black. I managed to build a fork with my knight after offering a gambit. Four moves later, I had his queen. He struggled and tried for the rest of the game, but I was in no mood to lose. We were the first ones to approach the bench to register our result. The person at the bench, an elderly man, smiled at me.

Game number four, I checked the lists and found that I was playing James Patterson in hall number 1. My heart thumped. A game in the main hall. Against a firangi! I'd never spoken to a white man ever in my life. Reluctantly I went into the main hall and took my seat. Exactly as I'd heard, this was a luxurious hall. Ceiling fans, marbled floor, polished furniture, uniformed servers.

A man approached me and said, 'Anand Sharma?'

I nodded.

'Come with me.'

Not knowing what the matter was, anxiously I followed him. I was scared, I surely didn't violate any rules. I hoped I wasn't being punished. I remember fellow players at other tables darting glances at me, casually, as I passed them. He took me all the way to the organizers' room where four Indians sat on a bench, behind a desk. Another man, a tall white man sat in a cushiony chair.

The man who had smiled at me earlier reconfirmed: 'Anand Sharma?'

I nodded.

He said, 'Hello, Anand. You had a pretty good run. Your next game is with James Patterson. You will play in this room against him. You are black. Good luck.' He pointed towards my back. I turned around to see who it was.

'A handsome guy, his golden hair well-oiled, fairer than Shweta, our whitest cow, wearing a bright shirt, a tie, blazer and grey trousers was sitting gracefully. His polished shoes shone like a mirror. I had never seen such a well-dressed person in my life. He must have been twice my age, and on his table was a bottled drink. His eyes gleaming with confidence, he had 'winner' written all over him. Brand-new pieces, shiny, carved out of wood, sat elegantly on a board made from rosewood, with a wooden clock on the left.

'I'm James,' he said. He did not shake hands – this was not unexpected. I looked at him. He had beautiful blue eyes.

I just shook my head. I forgot to introduce myself. What did I have for introduction anyway, other than my rustic look and clothes? I had the complexion of freshly tilled land – dark brown. To protect me from the cold, my mother had sewn me a shirt from bed linen. It felt thick and warm. Over that was a multicoloured sleeveless sweater that had no set pattern, and which my mother had knitted between tending to cows and preparing our meals.

I was in slippers, I didn't have a chess clock, my chess mat and pieces were old and pale. I felt like a page boy in the presence of a prince.

'Do you want to play with or without clock?' he asked.

My lips remained parted in awe of the grandeur he exuded. My heart was pounding and I was nervous. I kept nodding in response to whatever he said. Here I was, a green bean, from a village, first time ever in a city. How dearly I wished that my father was there with me.

I felt lonely and cornered in that room. I was reminded of a tiny paper boat floating in a flooded river. It was only a matter of time before it would go all squidgy and sink to the bottom.

He's not just a firangi but a special one to get such preferential treatment, I thought. My mouth was parched. If I could, I would have run away then. 'Dad, can I have a straw?' he asked, looking towards the white man in the chair. That man cast a glance at the organizers' desk where four Indians sat. One of them immediately got up and handed James Patterson a straw.

'Oh! So his father is the chief!' I thought. I wish my father was here too, committee member or not. I only ever saw him working in the fields, but he loved playing chess too, with an old ragged chess set he had inherited from his father. They often played under the village banyan tree, mostly after the harvesting was done. My father was an affluent farmer who owned acres upon acres of land. Tens of people worked for him. Then again, no matter how wealthy or honourable a villager might be, among the well-dressed and English-speaking folk, he would be no more than a 'villager'.

'Ready or what?' James said, interrupting my thoughts.

I was not ready, of course – I did not know how to operate a chess clock. I had never used the kind of scoring sheets he had on his side, details filled out, with a sharpened pencil resting on it. I was unprepared and under pressure.

'Umh.' Nothing else came out of my mouth.

He asked me to press a button on the clock to start the game. Nervously, I did. Tick-tick-tick-tick-tick-tick, my heart was racing faster than the clock; the red flag on the clock looked like a guillotine to me, waiting to drop freely on my neck. I was trying to look composed but my hands were not listening to me. He opened with the king's pawn. With a trembling right hand, I picked up my king's pawn to respond with the same move. It dropped out of my hand, fell on the board and rolled away on the floor.

'Oh you clumsy Indians!' he said, throwing his hands up in frustration.

I said sorry and bent down to grab the pawn and completed my move. He waited for a few seconds, looking at me.

'Do you even know how to use a clock?' he asked, disdain clear in his voice.

I shook my head.

'Why am I not surprised! You must press the button after making your move; otherwise your time will keep ticking. You'll lose on time and then you'll accuse us of playing unfairly. Plus, you must press the button with the same hand that you make your moves with.'

'Hmm.' I nodded.

My eyes were brimming with tears. Only my heart and my hands knew the state of my mind. Throughout, I forgot to close my mouth. Four moves later, I was a piece down. Another five moves, and it felt like I was playing reverse chess, as if I was handing him pieces out of reverence and devotion.

With each move, I got more nervous. Every time he lifted his piece, my heart pounded because I thought he would just announce 'checkmate' any moment. But there was no end to my suffering as he continued to butcher me and capture my pieces one after the other. I could have resigned and ended the game, but I was so nervous that I forgot I even had that option. After each move, I wiped my sweaty palm on my pants. I kept my hands under the table as much as possible.

When my time was ticking, I was doing everything other than focusing on the game. He must think I won the earlier three games by fluke, I thought. *What must the organizers think? I wish I were like him ... His clothes must be expensive.* He cleared his throat and I returned to the present moment. I wasn't sure what was more pathetic: my situation in the room or my position on the board.

I reminded myself to focus, but the game had deteriorated into a joke that had cost me a point and my self-esteem. He won in a matter of minutes where every minute had felt like an hour to me. I should have just not played from the outset. It would have looked more graceful, I felt.

My world had reached its end of time. I approached the bench to report the result. He stayed seated. Besides, everyone in the room knew the result anyway. My heart was no longer pounding; my thoughts were not racing any more. I was numb.

'0-1,' I mumbled with my head down.

I ran to the parking lot, got on my bicycle and just rode back as fast as I could. I did not have the courage to play the rest of the tournament.

I parked my bicycle on the unpaved road near our fields, leaving it unlocked, and ran over the ploughed land like an abandoned cow in a neighbour's farm. Father sat squatting, sowing the seeds. I threw myself at him and started crying.

'What happened? What's the matter? Are you okay?' he asked.

I just kept weeping, wetting his neck with my tears and snot. He started frisking me to make sure I wasn't hurt or injured. He ran his soiled hand through my hair to check if there were any wounds.

'Why are you crying? Did someone hurt you?'

I started crying even more loudly.

His hands touched my bag. He could feel the chessboard and chess pieces inside. 'Did you lose your bicycle?'

He separated himself from me using a little force, and put his hand under my chin to make me raise my head. I was sobbing. He wiped my tears.

'Tell me what's wrong, Nandu?' He called me Nandu affectionately.

'I lost.' My sobbing got louder.

'Okay, okay, calm down. In a game, one of the players has to lose.' He held me by my arm, lovingly, and took me to the nearby peepal tree. There was a raised platform around the trunk, which is where he and other workers in the field ate their lunch every day.

'Tell me now, what happened?' He sat down cross-legged, facing me, while I sat on the platform with my toes scraping the raw ground.

'I lost. He was a firangi. His father was the chief. He ... he had a special room. He was drinking cola too ... with a long pipe. He was very rich. He was dressed very ... very nicely. He had a brand new chess set. He had a chess clock with shiny glass. He had all the things I didn't have!' I said all this, choking, in a single breath, adding, 'Why didn't you come with me?'

Taking my hands in his big hand and caressing my head with the other, he said, 'Did he play with golden pieces?'

'What do you mean "golden pieces"?' I thought he was teasing me. 'I was black.'

'So, he played with white?'

'Yes.'

'Which means you did not lose to a firangi, you did not lose to some handsome guy, a prince or a king. You simply lost to white. He was playing on the same chessboard as you, with the same rules. It doesn't matter what he looked like or who he was. You were not playing against those things, you were simply playing against white pieces.'

Suddenly, I felt calm as well as incredibly stupid. I could not even understand why I'd felt the way I had at the tournament. It seemed unimportant now, immaterial who he was, what he was wearing or where he was seated.

'Promise me, Nandu, you will never let anyone intimidate

you. Ever. No one is going to come and wipe your tears out there. It's a rough world. Whatever the gimmicks, ultimately, the player who plays better wins. There are no two ways about it.'

I nodded.

'Be a lion. All right?'

'What's that on your shirt?' he pointed at my chest. As soon as I looked down he began tickling me. My laughter rang across the fields and I begged him to stop. He called out to one of the workers to carry on with the cultivation. Holding my hand, he took his bicycle and we walked until we were out of the fields. I sat in front, on the bar that joined the handle and the seat. His thighs would lift me one way then the other as he pedalled. The nearest shop was six kilometres away. We had cold jal-jeera and father got my favourite savoury biscuits with fennel seeds in it.

It wasn't for another four years that I met him again – James Patterson. The James Patterson. In all those years, I had already devoted a few thousand hours to chess. I was more confident in facing James. It was in the seventh round, that time. I could not win, but I didn't lose either; it was a draw. We had a face off again in the final round. I went all in. The fight was long and the tension nail-biting, but I was not prepared to lose. I too had a bottled drink on the table this time. His clothes, his white skin, his demeanour, polished board, the shiny chess clock, nothing mattered today. Managing to find a powerful line of attack, I triumphantly watched signs of anxiety emerge on his face. His game, just like his drink, was losing fizz as I continued to cement my position, eventually having the last word: checkmate.

Even though I would win many tournaments in the future, the feeling I experienced that day was like no other. It was as if I had banished a ghost from my past. It wasn't just winning against James Patterson. I felt I had won against my dark side, my own fears. I felt like the bird that just broke through the hard shell of an egg and caught a glimpse of a new world. I never played a major game without a soft drink on the table. Lemonade at first and then cola.

'ANYWAY, THE LESSON my father gave me that day, I pass on to you today, Vasu,' Master said most seriously. 'You ready?'

I nodded.

'Never let anyone intimidate you. Ever,' he said. 'You have as much right to your dreams as anyone else. You have as much claim over victory as the greatest out there. Never let anyone take that away from you, Vasu. Don't you *ever* let anyone intimidate you! You understand?'

I knew what he meant and I understood it too. Truth be told, a part of me was still intimidated. Glancing at his books alone, I thought it was impossible to win against someone like him. I felt like a tiny snowflake in front of a giant glacier. In fact, today I felt more scared than ever before. But I felt confident and secure as well. Not because I thought I would perform miracles, but because I just knew that I had found the best teacher there could be. And, sometimes, that's what makes all the difference – the one who's by your side.

4

SUCCESS BY DESIGN

IT WAS AN easy class – drawing. I didn't particularly like it though. I took it up only because I had to choose it over physical education. Why be out in the scorching sun and run around like a new recruit in the army when I could sit in a quiet room, like a sarkari babu, and doodle to my heart's content?

'Draw a winter landscape,' the teacher instructed. 'Today is a surprise test.'

How I hated those surprise tests! Not that the contents of a test that was declared in advance surprised me any less.

We called him Taklu – our bald drawing teacher. There was nothing artistic about him other than the neat baldness of his round head. And I never saw him laughing or talking nicely with anyone. Except with our general knowledge teacher, who was probably half his age.

I drew a wave with three swells. These were the mountains. Next came a semi-circle in the middle. My sun, hiding behind the mountains, of course. Underneath, I drew a little hut with a chimney sticking out like a sore thumb.

To add realism to my landscape, I tossed in some more circles to make a stone hedge for the garden. And then I sat there gazing at the circles.

Soft and fresh circular chapattis came to my mind. I was hungry and it was going to be lunch break after that period.

I didn't realize Taklu was standing over my shoulder, staring at me while I was running around in circles about my circles.

'Are you in grade three?' he bellowed.

I got up immediately.

'Sir?' I mumbled.

He picked up my drawing book and repeated the question. 'Is this what you draw in ninth grade?' The decibel level rose. 'You call this a landscape?'

For some reason, he always signed with a sketch pen. He pulled out a red one and drew a circle on my sheet.

'Zero,' he scoffed, slapped the drawing book on my desk and walked back to his.

I felt like jumping at him like a baby monkey and whacking his bald head with my drawing book. This visual disappeared when I realized the significance of zero.

One – the number of subjects I had failed in in the last six months. Two – times my father had been summoned by the principal. Three – warnings I had received for not paying attention in class. Four – subjects I barely passed. Five – 'get-out-of-the-class'es I got from various teachers. But, above everything else was the persistent zero.

Zero – the number of times I had hung out with my friends in the past few months. Zero – the number of days I had missed chess. Zero – weekends I just slept in. Zero – wins against the master.

Cipher. The sum total of my feelings and existence.

I knew the major openings like the back of my hand. King's pawn, Queen's pawn, Ruy Lopez, Gambits, Nimzo-Indian, Bird's opening, Semi-slav defence, Caro-Kann, Reti, Queen's

Indian, Sicilian, French, Grunfeld, Petrov, I had mastered them with the major lines of offence and defence.

But did this mean much, if anything? No. I still hadn't won against the master.

Even after thousands of games, I hadn't been able to get into his head. Even in my most carefully planned moves, he would seep in like water through the cracks. I couldn't predict his moves or counter his attack; the truth was, I couldn't do shit when playing against him. This wasn't just humbling, it was humiliating.

If chess was an ocean I was a castaway. The island, trees and shells in the form of attacks, exchanges and gambits in chess – none appealed any more. I felt like a drifting coconut bobbing up and down with waves as they carried me away from the island of my dreams into the muck of reality.

This blue ocean of chess was no longer beautiful but intimidating, a threat. My eyes were docked at the horizon, at some ship that would come to rescue me. But every ship my master sent was a pirate ship. Currently, the only thing I wanted more than a girlfriend was to win at least once. Just once. This would be the only way to rescue my fast-corroding motivation.

I got close to drawing on three occasions, but winning was nowhere in sight.

What's the point in chanting Hanuman Chalisa every day, Bajrang Bali? I'm still losing. That's not a fair exchange!

Why couldn't the master be a little kinder and let me win at least once? Was that too much to ask for? I didn't think so. That day again, we played and I lost, we played more and I lost more. If one win proved so difficult, how the hell would I win the hundreds required to be a GM?

'Will I ever win?' I asked him one day in the middle of a game, just after I lost my queen for his irritating knight that was jumping all over the board.

'Of course,' he said plainly. 'You will win when you are ready.'

'And I am not ready yet?' I flung the knight in the box. 'What about all the time I put in?'

'Vasu!' he bellowed. 'No one slams my pieces!'

'Not even one win against you!' I argued.

'Too bad.' Exhibiting no empathy or concern for my turmoil, he got back to his plain tone and pushed a pawn. 'Your move.'

Move? Does he really not care about how I'm feeling? His indifference threw me over the edge.

'You are so mean.' I growled. 'I am only fourteen!'

'Fourteen is young, huh?' he snorted with utter contempt in his voice. 'Chess is not for you. Go play marbles and don't show me your face again. You think someone will just hand you the game in real life? If you want it, you have to earn it.' He cleaned the board and chucked all the pieces in the box. For a moment, I was scared. But I was more mad than scared.

'I'm sick and tired of losing, losing and just losing,' I shouted. 'To hell with chess. I don't even like *you* any more.'

'Suit yourself.' I absolutely detested that indifferent tone of his. 'Chess is not for chicken.'

'Whatever. At least I won't be humiliated.'

'Haha! A beggar wants respect.'

'I am not a beggar!'

'Of course you are.' He rolled the chess mat. 'You want charity, not victory.'

'I hate you!'

'I told you the very first day, there's no magic pill, Vasu,' he said evenly. 'I thought you were champion material, strong enough to face defeat. I didn't realize you were a sissy. Let you win, huh!'

And then he went quiet. The silence was deafening. I wanted to storm out of there. But go where? I just sat there, blank and fuming.

Some time elapsed, I don't know how much, and both of us were staring at the chessboard. I didn't know what he was thinking.

'Even one win would have restored my confidence, you know,' I mumbled.

'Shall I serve it with cola, sir?'

'Give me a break, all right?'

'Go watch a circus, Vasu. Don't waste my time.'

'Okay, okay. Stop it! You don't have to be so cruel.'

I was struggling with my tears. First the losses and then his callous indifference.

Maybe he's right, I'm no champion material. My eyes welled up. I lowered my head and sobbed quietly.

He did not get up to pacify me. I threw a quick glance his way but he wasn't even looking at me. I sniffed and snorted while he kept staring at the table. The chess clock was still going tick-tick-tick-tick. He thrust an old cloth into my lap – the same one he would use to clean the chess pieces. I dabbed my tears and blew my nose.

'Make sure you wash it before you leave today,' he said.

I could hear the constant noise of kids playing in the street. Intermittent sounds of motorcycles, scooters, the tinkle of cycle bells would emerge at a distance, get louder and then trail off. It was the first time in the last six months that I paid any attention to the noise.

Part of me knew that he was right – no one out there would just hand me the game. I had to earn it.

'I'm sorry. I didn't mean to say those things,' I murmured. 'I didn't mean to shout.'

'Listen, son. If I go soft just to keep you happy, you will never learn the ways of the world or the game,' he said gently. 'To make good pots, a potter must knead hard to make the clay malleable. He must slap, pat and caress it with the right pressure at the right time or the pot will be useless.'

'Maybe I have been too hard on you. I have been living alone for forty-five years. I have lost touch with the world. I have mostly forgotten how to express my feelings. You're not wrong in not liking me.' He choked a bit.

I got up from my seat, pushed the chess table aside, and sat on the floor by his feet. Putting my head on his lap, I started crying again. The tears just came out.

'I'm sorry. You are the bestest in the whole wide world.'

He took off his glasses with his right hand and let it rest on the armrest, and patted my head softly with the left.

'I am thankful for everything you are doing for me. No one can be as kind and as loving as you,' I said.

'Don't make me all sentimental.' He took his hand off my head. 'I am worse then.'

Both of us chuckled.

'Never ask me to not show you my face again,' I said.

'Only if you promise to not spatter my trousers with your tears and snot.'

I giggled.

'All right, get up now. Let's get back to work. I will teach you Alekhine's Gun, a classic offensive strategy.'

He proceeded to set up the pieces as if nothing happened.

'Alekhine, huh?' he chuckled and looked lost in his thoughts.

'What about Alekhine?'

'Nothing.' He chortled.

Alekhine's Gun was named after the great Russian player and a former world champion, Alexander Alekhine. Even though I learnt the method, I knew it was not prudent to get my hopes up regarding my chances against the master. For a change, I was right – we played four games and I lost all four.

'I'm not complaining,' I said, 'but if I haven't won even once against you all these months, what chance do I really have of becoming a grandmaster, let alone a world champion?'

'Imagine building a hundred-metre long tunnel. Even at the ninety-ninth metre, when the end is only a metre away, you won't see any light. If you want success, you must go right till the end.'

'I do try my hardest. I try to go till the end. Still, I lose. Why?' I asked this question with the greatest composure, matching his plain tone.

'You are a genius, Vasu,' he said. 'I'm investing all my time in you because I know some day you'll surprise everyone, including yourself.'

My chest swelled with pride.

'And that day is not far,' he added.

I felt as if I had won the world championship. *He thinks I'm a genius!* I couldn't contain my smile and adjusted myself in my couch.

'But,' he said, gently bringing me down a notch, 'you are not consistent. You do play some brilliant moves, but they don't add up.' As always, he had a nugget of wisdom. 'Every move, Vasu, every move must put greater pressure on your opponent. To win, you must play good moves and do so consistently.'

'The same goes in life too,' he continued. 'A consistent and persistent man of average intelligence is more likely to succeed than an erratic and lazy genius. A hundred well-played draws, or a hundred lost but well-fought games are better than one victory by fluke. Success by design is infinitely better than a win by chance.'

Success by design is infinitely better than a win by chance – this got etched in my mind. This was it. The missing link. I had been playing in the hope that success would come, that it would just happen. It dawned on me that success was a sculpture that I had to carve and chisel at patiently. I had to design my success.

'All right, enough philosophy for now,' he said. 'Let's go out and celebrate!'

'Go out?' I exclaimed. 'Celebrate?'

'It's my birthday. I haven't celebrated anything in decades, but tonight I want to. We'll watch a movie, eat popcorn, drink cola, have a nice dinner and return late.'

'Why didn't you tell me?'

'I just did!'

'Besides,' he added, 'a good chess player is able to make and modify his plans at the last minute.'

'Fine! But no bicycle today,' I asserted. 'I'll drive and you will sit behind me, on my moped.'

'On a moped? No way. I've never sat on any two-wheeler other than a bicycle.'

'Today you will!'

He argued at length about the dangers of us falling down. What if someone crashed into his knees, what if I could not balance, what if this, what if that … But the argument wasn't taking place on a chessboard that he would just win; I didn't budge and he gave in eventually.

He put on the same old hand-knit sweater, same old trousers, everything looked antique and ancient, except his charming smile.

'Do I look all right?' he asked.

'What's this? You're always wearing the same clothes!'

'That's not true. I haven't worn this shirt in years.'

'And it's under your crocheted jumper! I can only see the collar.'

'Oh come on, it's okay. Let's go.'

'No! First you change.'

'Worry about what's inside, son. Only the inside matters for a good player.'

'Maybe, but we are not going for a tournament. We are going out for dinner. It's your birthday, we are celebrating! Please change.'

He went back to his room and came out ten minutes later.

'How do I look now?'

It was another crocheted jumper, the same shirt, similar-looking trousers, bright socks and, of course, the same shoes. But 'you look awesome now' is what came out of my mouth.

We had a blast. He was in a good mood and shared many of his childhood stories, how sometimes while helping his father sow the seeds, he would make piles of grains and start playing chess instead. How he would nudge his father to play chess with him rather than rest under the big peepal tree in the afternoons, and almost every time they did that, he would end up with some bird droppings on his clothes or on the chessboard. Each story had something to do with chess or a chess tournament. The more I heard him, the more I understood what he meant by eat, live, breathe, sleep chess. That's what he did. No matter what he talked about, it either began with chess or ended with it. If there were a curry called chess, he would order it for every meal.

Master was not just a teacher. He was a practitioner. He practised what he spoke about and he spoke about what he practised. He lived by what he stood for. His priorities were clear. His life had only one theme, he only lived for one passion – chess.

5

PLENTY OF FISH

A WHOLE YEAR passed. I was fifteen and even though I still hadn't won any game against the master, I was certainly improving. I had already won two tournaments, including the chess championship at school. They had started calling me the PC geek, for I always carried my pocket chess with me. If there was a break of more than five minutes, I would set up my board and start practising variations. My friends stopped playing against me because they had no chance of winning.

I only realized just how popular I was getting when a voice interrupted me in the middle of a chess problem one day. Our teacher was on leave and it was a free period.

'Vasu?' It sounded soft and too close to my ear.

I was abruptly pulled out of my chess world.

A pretty face with hazel eyes and thick eyelashes was smiling at me.

Jai Bajrang Bali. Help me, Hanuman. I gaped with my heart in my mouth.

Rea was gorgeous. And I was nervous, for good reason. It was only the second time in my fifteen years of unexciting existence that a girl had stopped by to speak to me. (The first time had been a disaster and that girl was not even half as cute as this one.)

'So, Kasparov,' she said, 'how are you doing?'

I wasn't pleased by her reference to Garry Kasparov because, even though he was young and emerging fast on the world chess scene, it was Anatoly Karpov who was the real chess champion. Anyway, I took heart from the fact that maybe she compared me to the world No. 2 because he was young and handsome, unlike Karpov who was a plain-looking bloke in his thirties.

'Good,' I said. 'I'm good. You?'

'Do you have a queen in real life too or you just keep knocking the one on the board?'

At first, I couldn't tell if she was joking or simply trying to carry on a normal conversation with me. Then she winked and smiled with a momentary raise of the brows. I was confused. As it was, I didn't think I would be of interest to anyone. I didn't exactly have the body of a wrestler or the panache of a cricketer. To be honest, I was just a gangly teenager who could easily pass off as a skeleton hanging in our biology lab.

Nevertheless, I went along.

'Of course, I'll have a queen by my side.'

'What if she doesn't want to be by your side?' she quipped. 'How will you lure her?'

'Well, miss,' I spoke with conviction, 'I've eight pawns to make eight potential queens.'

I smiled. She didn't.

I honestly thought I had given her a rather intelligent answer because if you can make it to the last rank in chess, you can turn any pawn into a queen. I thought she would appreciate the theoretical novelty of my response; any chess player would have. It was only after she'd rolled her eyes, said 'what a nerd' and stormed off that I figured it wasn't my best move.

That was that. I resolved to keep my focus limited to the queen on the board. She was enough for me, because all my dreams began and ended with chess.

But another day, she woke me up from that dream. A female voice was a welcome change. A real-life queen would certainly complete my world.

'Yes, Rea,' I said in serious tone. Hiding my nervousness and excitement.

I can't believe Rea wants to talk to me. Me! Rea! Everyone wants to talk to her.

'I wanted to talk to you in private,' she whispered.

'Sure. Me?'

'After school today? In the parking lot, near your moped?'

'Sure.'

Yahoo! She's certainly not going to be asking for your science notebook in the parking lot, Vasu. Yes, yes, it's what you think it is. Oh thank you, Hanuman. You rock!

'Here,' she said and handed me a folded chit.

She left quietly. Oh, how gracefully she walked, like a queen.

I opened the slip. In beautiful handwriting it was written: *You are the emperor of my heart.*

I forgot all about the chess problem and had a sudden urge to hold my chest, which was thumping louder than the gongs of Tibet. I rushed to the boys' room to check myself out. I was looking all right. I needed a haircut but other than that everything looked good. My shirt was ironed, my tie was gleaming, pants weren't crumpled and my shoes were polished. I took some water and combed my hair with my hand. My fingers smelled of coconut oil.

I don't know why mum insists on putting oil in my hair.
It had all run down to my face, which was shining like tinted glass. I took the hand soap and washed my face with it. I was smelling of fresh detergent, but I didn't have any perfume. I raised my hand to smell my underarms: the faint fragrance of rose talc was still there. I checked the other armpit too. Master had said average consistency is better than occasional brilliance, or something like that.

I wolfed down my lunch and vigorously rinsed my mouth. To be honest, I wasn't expecting any kisses, but I didn't want to smell like aloo-bhindi.

The next three periods crawled like a drunken snail. She was sitting in the third row, six desks ahead. I kept stealing a glimpse of her every now and then. She too gave me sidelong glances at the end of every class, topping them with a promising smile.

Everything just lit up. Butterflies were not merely flitting about tenderly in my stomach, they were razing my garden. I counted every moment. The last bell rang and I looked at Rea, and it seemed as if she blinked at me in slow motion. I ran to my moped and quickly cleaned its seat.

For the first time, I hated my moped. It was such a put-off. I wished Varun were there with his bike. Though old, he always kept it squeaky clean. I would have asked him to leave me with his bike for some time. I quickly checked myself in the side mirror of a bike parked nearby. The hair was a little unkempt and the oil had added its shiny gleam once again.

I sat on my moped and waited, but I was too restless, so I got down. I waited in the greatest anticipation, as if I were going to announce checkmate in my next move. Some ten minutes passed but she didn't turn up.

Maybe she's just fixing herself in the washroom. Oh these girls, they always take forever.

'Waiting for someone?' Two girls from my class asked as they pulled out their mopeds from the parking lot. They were Rea's friends.

'Umm ... no, not really.'

They whispered something to each other and laughed.

W-H-A-T-E-V-E-R.

Another ten minutes passed. The parking lot was getting deserted. There were still a couple of bicycles along with another moped. The last few kids were walking out of the school canteen. Rea didn't show up.

Maybe I should have asked those girls if they knew where Rea was. Perhaps she is waiting till everyone's gone. Wait a minute, the whole school knows she takes the school bus! Where is Rea? Maybe someone is coming to pick her up a bit later. But half an hour is already gone and she isn't here.

I thought of checking back in the classroom but what if she turned up at the bike stand while I went looking for her? It was a strange predicament. The watchman would come any minute and ask me to leave the school premises. Master must be waiting too.

Still, I couldn't leave without checking; so I walked back to D-block, which is where my classroom was, at least a few hundred metres away. Constantly darting glances in all directions, hoping to spot Rea, I was marching back to my classroom when Cadbury stopped me on the way.

'Where are you going, Vasu?'

'I ... I forgot something in the classroom, Ms Cadbury ... er ... Ms Claire.'

'What did you forget?'

'Umm ... my chess set.'

'There's more to life than chess, you know.'

Yeah sure, like the area of the moon?

'The rooms must be locked by now,' she said. 'Go home. You can get it tomorrow.'

'Maybe I could just check—'

'Vasu!' she asserted. 'I'm telling you that D-block is locked by now. Go home.'

With a heavy heart, I returned to my moped. I scanned it thoroughly to see if Rea had left any note. Nothing.

I didn't feel like playing chess that day. The first time in the last one year. I went home instead.

'Vasu!' mother exclaimed, surprised. 'You came early from your chess practice today!'

'I didn't go,' I replied.

'You didn't?' She paused. 'Did something happen at Mr Sharma's?'

'Mum!' I was irritated. 'I didn't go, I said!'

'Is everything all right?'

'Yes. Can you please not ask me any more questions?' I took off my shoes, left them there, went straight to my room and locked it from inside.

Thank God, Varun wasn't there. Because I wasn't up for any jokes.

I heard mum speaking to Master over the phone. She was telling him that I wasn't well and had come home straight.

Why didn't Rea come? I took out the slip and kept staring at it.

Mum knocked a couple of times asking about my lunch, etc. I just didn't open the door. I got up and fed Muffin, our goldfish. She was moving about freely in the bowl, eager to eat her food, oblivious to my misery. For four days, Muffin would stay at my desk and for three days at Varun's. Sometimes he would tease her by poking her bowl with his finger and I absolutely hated it.

'When she's on my desk, she's mine,' he would say and laugh.

'What if I poke you?'

'Try.'

'She doesn't mind, Munshiji,' he would say. 'The day she tells me to stop, I will.'

Muffin was rising to the surface presently, looking for more food. She was always hungry, but you had to feed her the right amount or she would fall sick. I kept alternating between watching Muffin and rereading the slip for the next few hours.

Dad was home and I could no longer keep my door locked. When he knocked around dinner time I finally opened the door. Everyone asked me what was wrong, but I wasn't going to tell anyone anything. I ate quietly and went back to my room.

Mum came into my room just when I was about to go to sleep. 'You know, Vasu,' she said, 'it's okay if you don't want to tell me what happened today but, just remember, it's not a kind world out there. It has many good people but it also has some unkind people who will hurt you. If you want to be happy and at peace, you must learn to protect yourself by believing in yourself.'

The next morning I left for school a little early, both anxious and eager.

There was a lot I wanted to say and ask Rea, but I knew I wouldn't be able to say it in person. I went straight to the library and wrote her a letter. My first letter ever. I poured my heart out and decided to hand it to her at the beginning of the first period.

The bell for the morning assembly rang. I kept searching for her. There she was, in the girls' queue.

Oh, she looked! And she smiled! My queen!

I wanted to jump high in the air. I felt like running up to the stage and singing a song.

Her friends, who were standing behind her, leaned forward and said something in Rea's ears. All three giggled, covering their mouths. I smiled at all of them. *Perhaps the other two also know how Rea feels about me.* I kept checking my pocket to ensure the letter was still there. It was not the sort of thing you would want anyone else to read, especially a teacher.

I rushed to the class as soon as the assembly got over. She had to have my letter. Now. There was no doubt about it: I was in love. I couldn't wait for the recess or till classes finished for the day. I was one of the first ones to enter the class.

There was some cursive writing on the blackboard. It was written in big letters, in yellow and fluorescent green chalk, with hearts and lips drawn in white and pink. Tendrils were drawn at the bottom-left corner. Someone, probably Rea and her friends, had taken pains to decorate the board for me.

> *On a moped a geek,*
> *A skinny chess freak,*
> *Always with his board,*
> *Here's a kiss for the toad.*
> *~ For Prince Alarming*

I had a momentary blackout. I thought I'd faint or fall. The other students were pouring in fast. I didn't even have time to rub it off without making a fool of myself. I went to my seat, which was towards the back anyway. Today it was particularly comforting that I had always been a backbencher. I wanted to disappear.

I was mad at myself for buying into her prank. It's not like I didn't know that she was out of my league. Every girl was, for that matter. I kept my head down.

'Good morning!' Our math teacher entered the class.

'Good morning, sir,' everyone chorused.

'Who did this?' he asked, pointing at the board.

It was no secret that it was written for me. I was the only skinny guy with a moped, the only chess freak.

The teacher asked again, angrier this time, but no one answered. He called a student to erase the board. I could have told him that Rea did it, I could have shown the slip, but I didn't want to be mocked a second time.

'Are you okay, Vasu?' He was standing next to me, his hand on my shoulder.

'Yes, sir,' I said more confidently than I actually was.

'Do you know who did this?'

I looked in Rea's direction. She was sitting in the first row. Like all other children, she too was looking at me. She lowered her head as soon as our eyes met. I ran my eyes over everyone.

'No, sir.' I could barely speak.

'Don't take it seriously,' he advised. 'Some people are insensitive cowards.'

I kept a tight check on my emotions throughout the day. At the end of every class, my friends would come and try to cheer me up. I acted as if it hadn't affected me. Every time I moved, the rustling of the letter in my pocket would remind me how dumb I had been. I didn't eat my lunch during recess, nor did I step out of class.

The day ended and I went home. I missed chess again.

'Munshiji has come,' Varun announced to mum.

I went straight to my room, with my shoes on.

They both entered after me.

'No chess today either?' she asked.

'I'm not well.'

She touched my forehead.

'Does he have fever?' Varun asked.

'No,' she replied. 'What happened, Vasu?'

'Nothing.'

'How will we know if you don't tell us?'

'Leave me alone!'

'My Munshiji is upset?'

I didn't answer. Varun and mum seemed to have reached a silent agreement that she leave the room.

Mother called my master again to let him know that I wasn't feeling well. Varun latched the door and sat next to me.

'Will you please tell me, Vasu?'

'I don't want to talk about it, Varun.'

'At least talk to me. I'm your brother.'

I just kept quiet.

'Do you want to take my bike for a ride?'

I shook my head.

He brought the fishbowl from his desk and placed it on mine.

'You can keep Muffin forever,' he said affectionately. 'One smile!'

I didn't react.

'Come on, let's go.' He held my wrist. 'I'll buy you a new chess set.'

I released myself from his grip.

'Tell me, Vasu.' He put his finger under my chin to lift my head. 'What's wrong?'

'And what will you do?'

'Try me.'

I pushed his hand away.

'Did someone bully you at school?' he guessed. 'Just say it and I'll break his kneecaps tomorrow.'

'No!' I shrieked. Varun was quite capable of it. He had a little gang of his own.

'Did Anand sir say anything?'

I shook my head.

'Are you in any trouble at school? Did some teacher scold you or something?'

'No, Varun, nothing of that sort.' I suddenly realized how much he cared about me.

'Wait a minute,' he exclaimed, 'I know it!'

I glanced at him to see if he really had guessed it, because he sounded so confident.

'You failed some exam, didn't you?'

'Noooo!'

'I've exhausted all possibilities, Vasu,' he said in a low voice. 'I can't see you like this, brother. Tell me what happened. I love you.'

It was something about those words – I love you – that melted my toughness and I started crying. Quietly.

He heaved a sigh of relief. 'Tell me now.'

'I can't, I can't.' My tears turned from a light drizzle into a waterfall.

Varun's face turned grave. He looked even sadder than I was.

'Is it about a girl?'

I kept quiet.

'It's about a girl, isn't it?'

I nodded. Only just.

'How did I miss it!' he exclaimed with joy. He clapped. 'Yes, yes, I should have known. Munshiji has grown up!'

I was mad at him for being so insensitive. I cursed myself for trusting him.

'That's all? You're upset because of a girl? Wait a moment. She dumped you, didn't she?'

I didn't think there was any point telling him that I had been ditched even before I was hitched.

'Do you know why I keep Muffin at my desk?' he asked.

'You said I could have her forever now.'

'Yes, yes, but do you know why I used to keep her at my desk?'

I had no interest in his dumb questions so I kept quiet.

'Come on, ask me why!'

'Why?' I asked.

'It's a reminder!'

'What reminder?'

He brought the bowl closer to me and asked me to put my hand in it.

'No, I'm not poking Muffin!'

'I'm not asking you to do that,' he persisted. 'Just put your hand in the bowl for a few seconds.'

'Why?'

'Just do it for my sake.'

'No,' I protested. 'Tell me why first.'

'I will tell you, I promise,' he said. 'Just put your hand in it.'

I did. And as soon as I did, Muffin swam to my hand thinking it was food. It felt nice to touch her.

'What did you feel?'

'Muffin.'

'Yes, but what's Muffin?'

'Fish.'

'Exactly, bro, exactly,' he said triumphantly. 'That's my point!'

'What?'

'Fish!' He pointed at the bowl. 'There's plenty of fish in the sea.'

My depression vanished with a poof and I laughed out loud. He was right. The haughty Rea was not the only girl on this planet. Someday, when I'd become a chess champion, she'd curse herself for playing the heartless prank on me.

'That's my Munshi.' Varun kept the bowl back. 'Don't waste your tears over some fish. Just keep the food ready and they will come in hoards.'

I couldn't stop giggling.

'Look at me,' he continued. 'I don't have any special talents, yet I have many girlfriends. And you are a chess prodigy, a sharp thinker. Girls – they like all this shit. They'll fall at your feet, my champion.'

I hugged him tight. So tight that I didn't want to let him go. Back in school, I had been thinking of ways to become invisible, including throwing myself from the school terrace. And now, none of that mattered. I realized that I'd missed two days of practice.

'Thank you, bro,' I said. 'I love you.'

'Let me go now,' he said. 'I'm not used to hugging guys.'

We burst into laughter.

'Do I still get to take your bike for a ride?' I mumbled.

'Umm ... okay.'

'And will you still buy me a new chess set?'

'You greedy monkey!'

'Let's go and do that right away.'

I tore up the letter and the slip – flushed them down the toilet with joy. It meant nothing. Varun and I went out for a ride, movie and dinner. He got me a rosewood chess set from his savings. How easily he erased my pain. *I love you, Varun.*

6

THE SOUL OF CHESS

I HAD GOT over the previous day's incident like a bad dream, but its memory was still vivid and my heart still sore. I rode a little slower and made it to school just in time. The blackboard was blank. I kept my bag in the drawer and left for the assembly. My eyes didn't seek out Rea. I got back in class to a surprise, though. Just as unexpected as the previous day's. In the last row, where I always sat, my bench partner wasn't the usual guy. Someone else had come even earlier and taken that spot – none other than the wicked Rea Joshi. Rea plot-hatching Joshi. The same Rea, who was never seen in any other row other than the first, was sitting on the last bench.

What does she want now?

Suddenly, my palms felt sweaty. My body tingled, as if a million ants were biting me. My heart was alternating between sudden spurts of excitement and quick bursts of anger. I was angry because I'd been humiliated. Or rejected. Cheated maybe. I couldn't tell.

The teacher still hadn't arrived. I hesitantly walked to my desk.

'H … Hi, Vasu,' Rea said in a sombre tone.

No, Vasu, don't even look at her. Have some respect. Show her you don't need her.

I don't know if she was smiling or not, because I didn't look at her. But my tone-deaf heart did skip a beat. It wouldn't listen to my reasoning.

I made a sorry attempt to not glance at her. It was like spotting a beautiful, hand-carved rosewood chess set in a shop, but looking the other way since you know if you stay there for any more than a few seconds, you will want it so desperately that you wouldn't mind stealing it. Your mind will keep hovering around it like bees around a flower. So, the best thing is to not treat yourself to that visual and mental feast. That's the only way to avoid the mess.

With a stern look, I opened my drawer, picked my bag and occupied another desk – the corner-most one, which was almost always vacant because it was a bit rickety. Right now, it matched my own condition.

'Vasu? I'm sor—' She called from behind but I ignored her. Once again, my heart knocked hard, but I held my fort. It felt strangely empowering to ignore and dismiss her, even though she was right there.

The day passed agonisingly slowly. I skipped lunch and immersed myself in chess during breaks. Rea continued to be at the back of my mind. *Maybe I should have sat with her. Maybe she wanted to apologize. What if she was playing another prank on me? What if she never approaches me again?*

It was time for the last class – drawing period. When it came to drawing, Taklu was not the only inconvenient factor; there was the drawing book itself. It was larger than any other book. I hated carrying it because it was always protruding out of my bag. So no matter how hard I tried to protect it, it would be all deckle-edged in a matter of days. And Taklu would unfailingly remind me that I was careless. I'd never ask my parents to spend 300-odd rupees on a bigger school bag just to please my drawing teacher.

I pulled out the monster book and something slipped out and fell on the floor. It was a letter. From Rea. She must have slid it in the morning, immediately after the assembly. *What a lovely thing, this drawing book. It's so good that it sticks out, inviting important letters.*

I looked in Rea's direction. She was looking at me as if she was waiting for me to read the letter. I contemplated tearing it up to show her I didn't care. But, of course, this was a fleeting thought. In the most beautiful handwriting, was written:

My dear Vasu,

Only I know how I mustered up the courage to sit next to you today. I'm really sorry for yesterday and the day before. If you believe me, it wasn't my idea but, dumb that I am, I just got carried away.
I know it sounds really crazy. I know. But with this terrible prank, I at least got your attention. I am very sorry.
There's much I want to say to you. I'll wait for you, Vasu, hoping that one day you will sit next to me.
Love ya!
Yours
R

P.S. Please don't share this letter with anyone. Please.

'Vasu?' Taklu roared. 'What are you reading?'

'Nothing, Ta …, er, sir.' I quickly stuffed the letter in my pocket.

'I called out three times! What have you got there?'

'No, sir. Nothing, I mean.'

'What, no sir?' He came closer and pulled my hand out of my pocket.

'Sir!' I screamed. 'It's a personal letter!'

'Not in my class!' He made another attempt to reach my pocket.

'Sir!' I pushed his hand away with all my might. 'This is none of your business!'

A strange hush fell in class.

'You are coming with me to the principal's office, right now!'

I stood there quiet but no less mad.

I glanced at Rea. Her face had turned ashen, like mine had been the previous day. 'Now!' He was already at the door, yelling.

At the principal's office, Taklu dramatized every action of mine, saying how he stepped away in time to avoid me shoving him to the ground, etc. He tried to convince her that no warning or meeting with my parents was necessary and that an expulsion letter was the only viable option. I was a bad influence on other students, according to him.

The principal, however, wasn't blind to Taklu's tendency to overreact. The school needed me. I was its chess champion and would soon represent the school at the national level. However, disregarding a teacher's complaint wasn't going to set the right precedent either.

'You are placed under suspension for one week, Vasu,' the principal said. 'This won't go on your record, but it is our final warning.'

Taklu had a contented smirk that neither I nor the principal missed. I begged her pardon and asked for a last chance, but she wasn't willing to entertain any more pleas.

'My office will issue you a letter,' she said. 'You can collect it in the next ten minutes.'

'Can you please allow me to skip drawing and switch to physical education?'

'Not this late into the session.'

It was over. She indicated that I could leave.

'Thank you,' I murmured and walked out to get my bag.

'And Vasu,' she said from behind, 'as a mandatory step, we'll call your parents for a meeting to inform them in person.'

'Yes, ma'am.'

I closed the door. I felt sorry that my parents would have to go through all this, but I wasn't feeling humiliated or bad for myself. Perhaps it was just because I was young. Perhaps it was Rea's letter.

Master had said that the greatest chess players attained maturity of thought early on in their life. It's a natural outcome of playing a thought-intensive game. But surely, thinking doesn't make your raging hormones subside?

When you're in your teens, something nudges you to rebel at things you don't even want to. You don't want to get angry but anger is all that comes out. Half your time goes in feeling upset and guilty that you are not good enough. You curse yourself for procrastinating, for lashing out, for not following a discipline. And for the rest of the time, you are trying to please your friends, parents and teachers. You want them to acknowledge, recognize and appreciate you. You want attention and recognition. It's very gratifying. But most of what you try doesn't work.

You want to but you don't really give a shit about a lot of things. So: to hell with school. I began thinking of intensive chess sessions with the master over the next week.

Trrriiinng. I stood outside Master's house, waiting to ring it two more times because, for reasons best known to him, he always opened at the third ring.

'Vasu!' He opened it right away.

Rather than the usual touching-of-feet ritual, I went for a hug. I wasn't sad nor did I need any support; I did it merely to express my love. When I saw him, I realized that I had missed him. He hugged me back, not as hard as I'd hugged him, though.

'Can you please speak to my mother and tell her that I'm okay?' I said. 'The school must have called home by now.'

'What happened?'

I narrated the events that had begun two days ago as a prank and ended with my suspension. He stroked my head. I showed him Rea's letter even though she had asked me not to show it to anyone. I couldn't hide anything from the master. I didn't want to.

'I'm sorry to hear that, Vasu,' he said affectionately. 'Are you sure you are okay?'

'Honestly, Master, I'm not worried. I didn't do anything wrong.'

He called mum and told her not to worry about me and that he would come home in the evening to meet them.

'Did you eat your lunch?' he asked.

'Did mum ask you to ask this question?'

'No!' He chuckled. 'Let's eat it together now. I haven't had anything since morning either.'

'Since morning? Why?'

'I wasn't feeling too well.'

'Why? What's the matter?'

'Nothing. Just like that.'

There was no point pushing him further because he rarely

said anything he didn't want to. Besides, I thought he might have missed his breakfast just like I missed my meals every now and then.

We made some instant noodles, which took all of twenty minutes, not two, like the packet claims. Master was coughing. Not too much or too loud. I was worried but didn't want to pester him.

'I'll get the cold drink,' I offered.

'I'm not sure if I should have one,' he said after a brief pause.

'No cola?' I couldn't believe my ears. 'How can that be?' He must be feverish, I thought.

'Okay, I'll have one.'

He probably agreed in order to shut me up from asking more questions. We ate our noodles and drank cola. He never liked talking or doing anything else while eating. Other than his occasional bouts of cough, it was a quiet but good lunch. Anything and everything was good in the master's company.

'Are you sure you are okay to play today, Vasu?'

'That's exactly what I was going to ask you!'

'Why? I'm okay.' He shrugged.

'Me too.'

'You know, I thought with all that happened in school and all—'

'Nah,' I said cockily. 'I can handle that.'

He quietly spread the chess mat and told me that, over the next week, since I had no school, we would replay the games of the grandmasters from *Chess Informant*, the bi-yearly publication that featured all the games of the grandmasters in all the rated tournaments across the world.

'Do you know who the finest teacher is?' he asked.

'You!'

Ignoring my answer, he continued, 'Experience is the greatest teacher, Vasu. Always replay your own games to see where you went wrong and what made you play the way you did. People don't lose because they make mistakes, they do so because they repeat their mistakes. The first time, it's not a loss but a learning.'

'So, how do I avoid making mistakes?'

'Just don't repeat them,' he said after coughing and clearing his throat. 'Be it life or chess, that's the only difference between a grandmaster and an amateur. An amateur expects to reach a different destination by walking the same path. He hopes for miracles or serendipities. A grandmaster, on the other hand, relies on his own effort and intelligence. He does not commit the same error twice.'

'But Master,' I said, curious, 'I do try my best to not repeat my mistakes. Why do I still lose?'

'Because you nourish the body and starve the soul.'

I gave him a blank look because I didn't have a clue about what he just said.

'Do you know the soul of chess, Vasu?'

'Winning?'

'The soul of chess is pawn play.'

He resumed after a brief silence. 'You can retreat any piece but a pawn. That position, once lost, never comes back. Over the next seven days, I want you to pay attention to how grandmasters play with their pawns. I want you to understand how they treat their pawns.'

Suddenly, many of my own games flashed in front of me, where I had just pushed a pawn impatiently because I couldn't really figure a way out. I was reminded of many games where my own king or pieces had remained blocked behind my own pawns. In fast-forward, my mind replayed many games where Master had won because I couldn't go past his pawns.

Of course, that's it. Pawns.

'Today is not about chess, though,' he sounded sombre. 'Because, there's life beyond chess, Vasu.' He waited a moment before continuing: 'Chess is not about winning. It's about playing. The high you feel in victory is only there because of the tension of the game during the play. If you beat a much less skilled opponent without any struggle, the victory won't be as fulfilling. That's how it is in life too. Our obstacles and adversities add to the euphoria of triumph.'

'Are you saying chess is like life?'

He laughed. 'There's no comparison, Vasu. Chess has rules, life has none.' Then he added, 'Besides, chess is a part of life and not the other way around.'

It was the first time he suggested that anything could be more important than chess. I couldn't quite figure out why, though.

'Do you know why your drawing teacher is always angry?'

'Because he loves to see others suffer. He's not a Taklu, he's a poisonous berry.'

'No point in speaking ill of a person, Vasu,' Master said in his usual plain tone. 'He's angry for the same reason as you losing in chess repeatedly.'

'You mean he is nourishing his body while his soul is starving?'

'Exactly. What is the soul of life?'

I shook my head.

'Love, Vasu, love,' Master spoke. 'Love is the soul of life. Without love, nothing has any meaning nor value. Your drawing teacher needs love.'

The first thing that came to my mind was how happily Taklu exchanged pleasantries with the GK teacher. Leaning on the staff room door, with a smile that seemed to be reserved for her, he would move his hands like a robot on Duracell batteries, sharing jokes and anecdotes with her.

'But I don't feel any love for Taklu.'

'Not if you keep calling him Taklu. Do you like it when they call you a geek?'

Sensing where he was going with the conversation, I said, 'I don't call him Taklu to his face.'

'That doesn't matter, Vasu,' he replied. 'What we call someone behind their back is how we see them. That's how they shape up in our mind. Your drawing teacher is trying to do his job. Labelling others based on their appearance is a sign of mediocrity and pettiness.'

I felt bad, even ashamed, of myself. How conveniently I'd been referring to Ms Claire as Cadbury, and Mr Goyal as Taklu, and there were many other not-so-nice nicknames assigned to others. But just one reference to me as a geek or a chess freak and I was totally shattered. Master had just shown me a mirror.

'And let me tell you something,' he said, cutting into my thoughts. 'Mediocre behaviour is not befitting of great people. Just like average play doesn't lead to winning in chess, average demeanour does not lead to great things in life.'

'I feel like a really bad person.'

'You won't if you learn to feed your soul,' he replied. 'On that note, if love is the soul of life, how do you feed it?'

'By loving others?'

'Yes, but what does that mean?'

As usual, I shrugged. What did I know about love? I thought giving my mother a hug was an expression of love. I thought being friends with Rea would be something like love. Maybe playing chess was loving ... or cracking jokes with Varun was. It was a feeling I had felt for all these people but not for Mr Goyal or the indifferent security guard at my first chess tournament.

'Love is to feel good about the other person,' I replied nevertheless.

'Not quite,' he sipped his cola and coughed. '*Forgiveness* is love. Acceptance *feeds* love. When you accept the other person the way they are, you begin to respect how they are. You begin to value what matters to them. Forgiveness for their mistakes arises naturally. Love blossoms like a lotus upon sunrise then. And when you are in love, everything feels all right. No matter how life actually is, it just feels right.'

'How do I forgive my drawing teacher?'

'By seeking his apology first.'

His answer upset me. It didn't make sense.

'Hadn't you already labelled him Taklu before you even got to know him?' he said as if he'd read my mind. 'Love starts by taking responsibility for our own actions first, Vasu. Write him a sincere apology. Set your karma straight first, Nature will take care of his. When you beg his pardon for your thoughts and conduct, love will flow from you. Basking in your love, he will undoubtedly feel love for you in return.'

Master was coughing even more. He got up to spit.

Like a carefully crafted chess strategy, his wisdom penetrated all my defences. I decided to not only write an apology to Mr Goyal but also go to school the next day to deliver it in person.

'What about Rea?' I asked as soon as he sat down. 'What do I do with her?'

'Forgive her. Accept her.'

'And let me tell you something more,' he said. 'Rea is a keeper.'

'Really!' I couldn't contain my surprise. 'How do you know?'

'Well, let's say, your master has played enough games to sense if the queen is going to hang around till checkmate. Though, a gambit is more important than a checkmate in love.'

I wasn't exactly sure what he meant.

'Because Vasu,' Master continued philosophically, 'love is not about winning but offering. The first gambit is care, second appreciation, but it's the last gambit that matters the most.'

'And that would be?'

'Self-sacrifice. Until you offer yourself wholeheartedly, you can't win. In love or in anything else.'

We didn't play any games that day but only examined various end-game permutations. I wasn't distracted but I couldn't really focus either. There was plenty on my mind but I was mostly dying to tell Rea that I would like to sit next to her in class.

With all its challenges, one of the most beautiful things about the teenage years is love. It's so easy to fall in love when you are growing up. Maybe because you are so sure of everything, or because you want to give yourself to someone. There's so much to look forward to. Although, it could just as easily be because you are a green bean and don't know any better.

Whatever it might be, today I felt like a winner. I felt big for my own shoes. I was willing to apologize to Taklu. Yes, I could call him that this one last time. Rea said she wanted me. I felt victorious. A champion – albeit on a one-week suspension.

7

WHEN MASTER CALLS

'**M**UM!' I SHOUTED as soon as I got home.
'Sshh...' she whispered. She looked grave. 'Your father is really angry. They called from your school.'

This was some serious shit because father rarely ever got mad; but when he did, he would lose it completely. No one in the family had forgotten how hard he had slapped Varun four years ago. My brother had already failed in two exams but father had not lost his cool. But soon Varun had bunked school for a whole week and submitted a leave of absence forging father's signature. No one had found out. Theoretically, it was not a bad plan but it had backfired when Ganju uncle had turned up at home.

Ganju uncle was not just anybody. Even though he sat at home and never really worked while his wife slogged in an accounts office, raising a family of four, he was an expert at transport – of packets of information.

We used to call him AIR – short for All India Radio. That day, he had his share of tea and biscuits and, when he was about to leave, he casually dropped a bomb saying he saw Varun loitering around a B-grade cinema hall on two occasions in a single week. We all turned to Varun who denied the accusation vehemently.

'But I saw you eating a samosa, beta,' he said unctuously. 'You were in your school uniform.'

And what were you doing at a B-grade movie hall, uncle?

Dad had dismissed uncle saying that he must have been mistaken, but he quietly made enquiries at the school to get to the bottom of the matter. All hell broke loose when he found out the truth. The slap was so hard that Varun's face got bruised and he had fallen on the floor. Dad had helped him up, but Varun cupped the left cheek to avoid getting another. He was no Mahatma Gandhi to turn the other cheek – which didn't stop dad from delivering a resounding slap on the other side. With his left hand, this time.

Varun had wisely run away and spent two days at his friend's place until dad calmed down and called him back.

'Vasu, after I got the first slap,' Varun would recount later, 'it felt as if the temple priest was blowing a conch in my right ear. The next one landed and it was Bismillah Khan playing shehnai into my ear with various accompaniments. I felt I was on another planet, maybe dead, and celestial beings were all around me, like fireflies. In the middle of all that stood our father, glaring at me, like the mighty Ravana at the helpless Sita. Hey Ram!'

I had no friend like the one who had given Varun shelter. I could go to Master's house but I wasn't comfortable exposing that side of my father.

'Vasu!' A loud, angry voice sent a chill down my spine. I trembled like a dry leaf at the sudden gust of wind. I seriously thought of turning back and running away. But it was a little too late for that.

He was already here, my father. Angry, mad, red-faced. In one jerk, he took my school bag off my shoulders. It twisted one of my arms but this was the least of my concerns presently. He tore open my bag and took out the chess set. With one hand, he flung the bag on the wall. He dragged me by the wrist and went to the veranda. With all his might, he slammed the chess set on the floor. Its hinges broke in an instant and cracks appeared.

I stood there in shock. Mother was standing in a corner, looking petrified, Varun and Mira beside her.

He sat on the floor and put his hands on his head.

I thought the storm had passed. I didn't realize that it had been building up in him the whole day. This was just the sea retreating before the giant tsunami. Completely unaware and mistaking his current posture as an indication of calming down, I went little closer. It was a big mistake.

'I'm sorry, father,' I murmured.

'No, you are not sorry,' he roared. 'You bloody little rascal.' He was yelling. 'Where do I go, God? What do I do with these dirty eggs? I damn the day I ever became your father. I damn the day you were born. You guys think life is a walk in the park. It's all easy, a bed of roses.'

He got up and picked Varun's cricket bat. 'You are dead meat, Vasu.'

I saw not my father but death looming large. I was so terrified of him swinging the bat at me that I shrunk in fear, cupped my head with my hands, and didn't move an inch.

Mother immediately sprang to stop him.

'You are not touching him!' she roared.

Taken aback by her sudden intervention, without a word or warning, he pushed her away. In an effort to regain her balance, she tried to hold on to something, but her saree got stuck in her big toe, and she toppled and fell back on her head. There was a loud thud as her head hit the concrete staircase. No other sound came from her.

'Ma!' Varun leaped to pick her up. But there was no movement. He sat down and put her head in his lap. Blood was oozing out non-stop.

'Mum!' Mira screamed. She was trying to wake her up.

'Anu?' Father grabbed her pulse to check it. 'Anu, please wake up. I didn't mean to hurt you.' He was choking, breaking out into a sweat.

Mum lay there unconscious. A terrible thought flooded my mind: what if she never woke up. No, I couldn't think like that. I wanted to move closer and touch her, shake her, but I was just rooted to the ground. It felt unreal, like a nightmare.

It didn't feel like home any more. It felt more like I was just walking on the road and people had gathered around a stranger who had been in an accident. I looked at mum. Father, Mira, Varun, they all looked like strangers – I didn't know them. They were trying to bring her back to consciousness, but she wasn't responding.

'Vasu! Vasu!' Father shook me. 'Get some water!'

I stood there, paralysed.

'What's wrong with you, Vasu?' he shouted at the top of his voice. 'Get some water. Now!' He shook me violently.

I neither moved nor cried.

Mira ran to the kitchen and got a glass of water. He sprinkled some on mum's face. 'Please get up, Anu,' he cried. 'I'm sorry.'

There was no movement. Not even so much as a twitch. Father grabbed a t-shirt hanging on the clothesline and tied it on her head to prevent further blood loss. Lifting her in his arms, he ran barefoot. We had no car, and ambulances in our small town were used more often to transport groceries for various officers. Patients were expected to make it on their own.

'St. John's Hospital,' he yelled. 'Lock the house and reach there.'

How tiny she looked in my father's arms! It was strange to see him carry her like that. How effortlessly he held her, tenderly but protectively. There was not a sign of the anger that had distorted his face just a few minutes earlier. His eyes were full of fear, though: fear of losing her.

The hospital was about eight kilometres away. At the end of the street, you could usually find an autorickshaw or two. Like a mad-man, he ran out with mother in his arms. I wasn't sure if she was dead or alive, whether I would ever hear her call me Vasu again. I had no clue if she would worry about my food again. I didn't know what the future held for us.

'Let's go, Vasu,' Varun howled. He had just washed his hands; his shirt and jeans were still smeared in blood. He was holding father's wallet.

'I need a minute,' I said calmly. It only came out that way. I wasn't calm at all.

'We don't have a minute,' he shouted back. 'Don't you understand? It's all happening because of you.'

'Shut up, Varun!' Mira chided him. 'It'll be okay, Vasu,' she said softly. 'Let's go.'

'I just need a minute, Mira.' And without saying another word, I ran into my room.

There he was, Hanuman, with his mace on his shoulder, smiling. He seemed so oblivious to what had just transpired, so unconcerned.

'O Bajrang Bali,' I lifted him in my palms and touched his feet to my forehead. 'It's okay if you never grant me another wish, but don't take my mother away. Bajrang Bali, please don't take my mother away. I promise I'll behave and be a good boy. Please, God, please let her live. I beg you.'

In a blinding flash, shorter than the fraction of a moment, I saw a vision. A vision of the future. Vasu Bhatt with his mother on a stage, receiving the trophy for the world championship. There was thunderous applause all around. In my heart of hearts, I felt this was a real vision. Time could not take away my mother just yet. I knew Hanuman would protect her. A new energy surged through me. I quickly wiped my eyes that were welling up and ran out.

'Mum will be fine, trust me,' I hollered and flashed the little idol of Hanuman in my hands as if he would actually speak to them or show them what he had just shown me. They said nothing. We rushed to the hospital.

'She's still unconscious,' the doctor said. 'We can't tell how bad the injury is until we see the scan.'

Mother got eight stitches on her head. They put her on drip.

Father was running barefoot from one department to the other to organize all the necessary tests. It wasn't easy to get things done in a hospital owned by a charitable trust and partially funded by the government. Two hours later, her report was with us.

'There's internal bleeding,' the doctor said. 'We'll have to operate. But the chief neurosurgeon is gone for the day. We'll keep her under observation. The surgery will be done tomorrow.'

'Can't it be done today?' father asked.

'No,' came the indifferent reply. 'It'll be done tomorrow.'

'Tomorrow?' father argued. 'We can't wait till tomorrow. Why can't we call the chief surgeon in this emergency?'

'We get emergencies like this every day,' the doctor said, a little irritated, while checking mum's blood pressure. 'We can't just call him.'

'What if it were your mother dying here?' Varun screamed. 'You piece of shit!'

'Watch your mouth or I'll have you thrown out of the hospital,' the doctor said, pointing his finger at Varun.

Mira pacified Varun. She said something to him but I wasn't paying attention. I was looking at mum. She was just lying there as if nothing had happened, unaware of everything that was happening around her. I gripped the Hanuman idol again.

Father went to the officer-in-charge but he gave the same reply – the chief surgeon could not be called at that hour. Father made some calls to find out if anyone could do anything. It was a small town and everyone knew everyone else. Yet no one seemed to know the chief surgeon.

I took a five-rupee note from my father's wallet and walked to the PCO just outside the hospital and dialled a number.

'Master?' I said in a low voice.

'Vasu?'

I burst into tears.

'What happened, Vasu?' His voice was so comforting, just like mum's.

I told him about what had happened and how the chief neurosurgeon wasn't available for surgery. Master reconfirmed if my mum was admitted at St. John's hospital.

'Yes, she is.'

'Go tell the doctor to prepare the OT. The chief surgeon will show up in the next twenty minutes.'

I couldn't believe my ears. More tears rolled down.

'Everything's going to be all right, Vasu,' he spoke reassuringly. 'Go now. I have to make a call.'

'Four rupees and twenty paise,' the PCO owner said as soon as I put the receiver down. I just placed the full five rupees in his hands and ran to the hospital.

'Your change,' he shouted from behind.

It was already 8 p.m., well past the visiting hours. We were not allowed to see mother even from outside the ICU.

Father and Mira were still sitting outside the doctor's room, looking desperate. Varun was pacing the corridor madly.

I barged into the doctor's room. Father followed behind. Mira and Varun too.

He was livid to see me … us, enter like that.

'What do—'

'Master says get the operation theatre ready. The chief surgeon will be here in a matter of minutes.'

'What master?' he said. 'Who?'

'My master, my chess teacher.'

He snorted as he chuckled. 'On any other day, it might still be a possibility. Not today,' he scoffed. 'It's his daughter's sixteenth birthday. Every bureaucrat in the city has been invited. Half the hospital staff is there.'

O Hanuman! What is he saying?

'Master doesn't lie.'

'Listen, kid,' he said gravely. 'I'm in the middle of some important work. Wait out—'

Tring … tring. Tring … tring. His phone rang.

'Hello!' he shouted into the phone. 'Yes … yes, yes, sir, right away.' His voice got lower with each yes.

'Yes, sir,' he continued, 'Loss of consciousness. Yes, sir. Traumatic brain injury, sir. Yes, sir … Subdural hematoma, sir … Sure sir, BP, pulse, okay … sir. Yes, sir … I thought I couldn't call you. But, sir—'

I could hear a beep from the other side.

He put the phone down, got up and took his gown off the hook.

'Dr D'Souza will be here in ten minutes,' he said hurriedly. 'Who did you say your master was?'

'I didn't say.'

'What's his name?'

'Not telling you.'

He gave me a dirty look and rushed out to get the OT ready. The hospital, which was deserted like a cremation ground until a few minutes ago, was suddenly bustling with activity. The staff was getting ready. I could hear shouts of a number of medical terms: bandage, drip, knife, power backup, meds...

Varun lifted me up in elation. 'Your master is a magician, Vasu!'

A ray of hope, a feeling of great relief flitted across father's face.

Mother was shifted from the ICU to the OT and Dr D'Souza reached in practically no time.

We were given staff canteen vouchers for our dinner, but nobody ate. The surgery went on for over two hours.

'Vitals are okay,' Dr D'Souza said. 'But it's only after her consciousness returns that we'll know the prognosis. She'll be under observation for the next three days.'

My father thanked him profusely for leaving the celebrations midway and coming to do the surgery at such short notice.

'What could be a greater celebration than saving a life!' he said. 'Whether I look at it as a Christian or as a doctor, either way, it's my priority.'

Our saviour then dashed out as speedily as he'd arrived. His guests were probably waiting for a late-night celebration with him.

Mother was shifted back to the ICU. Varun went home with father to change his clothes. About time too; with his crew-cut, his solid build, and the blood smeared across his shirt, he had looked like an off-duty soldier caught in the middle of a siege.

Hanuman was still safe in my hands. Or was I in his? Father came a little while later and asked us to go home and get some sleep. Both Mira and I refused. We were not leaving till Mum opened her eyes, we said. He tried to reason but we did not relent. The whole night passed very slowly, very quietly. We slipped in and out of sleep in the waiting room.

Dawn broke, the sun rose and the hospital was buzzing again. It was a different place now. Not that a hospital is a desirable place at any time of the day, but a night in a hospital is a completely different affair. It seems to foreshadow death with its doom and gloom. In the morning, you look up to life once again.

Only one visitor was allowed in the ICU at a time. One by one, we visited mother. Mrs Anu Bhatt. I tried talking to her but she did not respond. Sixteen hours had passed since she fell and she still hadn't moved or opened her eyes. The doctor said all we could do was wait.

Master visited during the day but he was coughing throughout. He asked me how mum was and walked straight into Dr D'Souza's office. I caught a glimpse of the doc getting up instantly, like a sergeant would at the entry of a general, and the door closed behind my master. He came out after a few minutes and didn't say a word. When I asked him out of courtesy to go home since he was unwell, he promptly left, without offering to stay back at all.

I was too worried about my mother to reflect on anything though. Father and Mira tried to feed me, but I didn't eat. I was waiting for the next window of time when we could see mum again. We would press our faces against the glass to catch a glimpse of the corridor of the ICU. Every time anyone walked out, we would ask about mum.

Evening came and we were allowed to visit her again. I was the last one to go in this time. I wanted to be with her, but I was scared to see her like that. Unlike my mother who couldn't ever have enough of me, the pale figure on the bed did not talk to me at all.

It was late evening. The silence of the night was setting in again. The cardiogram was flashing her pulse and some other numbers. It was utterly quiet. An intravenous tube was taped around her left hand. Every now and then there would be a beep. It meant that all was okay. Her lips looked particularly dry.

I kissed her face. It was warm.

'I'm sorry, mum.' I stroked her face but she didn't respond. Any other time, she would have melted right away. She would have asked if I had slept properly the previous night, if I had eaten during the day.

A tear trickled down my eyes and fell on her face. There was no reaction from her. I gently wiped it with my thumb.

'Your Vasu is hungry, mum,' I whispered in her ears. 'I haven't eaten since yesterday.'

Her body twitched. Only just, but it did. Her eyes were still closed, but the eyeballs seemed to move.

'Yes, mother,' I repeated. 'Your Vasu is hungry and won't eat without you.'

Her eyelids folded slowly. She was looking at me, trying to focus. She looked around. The first few seconds went by as she tried to recall how she could possibly have ended up on a hospital bed. She was about to speak but I placed my hand on her mouth. I wasn't sure if it was okay for her to talk.

'Please wait,' I said. 'I'll get the doctor.'

She realized that there was a drip running through one of her hands. She raised her other hand to her mouth. Joining four fingers with her thumb, she gestured to me to eat something. I ran out crying, calling out for the doctor and my father. The image of my mother's gesturing me to eat would remain etched on my mind for the rest of my life.

8

MY MOJO

'WHEN WILL ANU be discharged?' Master called on the third day. I happened to go home to change into a fresh pair of clothes and that's when the phone rang. It wasn't his question but his tone that surprised me. It was plain as usual. When it came to my mother, I was hoping he would be a bit more compassionate. Nevertheless, I was pleased to hear his voice after three days.

'Good morning, Master,' I said. He kept quiet.

'They'll discharge her on Monday.'

'And what about chess?'

'I was planning to resume next week.'

'Vasu,' he said, as usual, plainly, 'your first rated tournament starts in two weeks' time. You can't afford to miss your practice.'

What is he talking about? Chess over my mother?

'But,' I protested, 'mum's still in the hospital. My *mother!*'

'Do you think your mother will be happy to have you in the hospital and lose the tournament?'

'But she needs me!'

'What are you, a doctor?' he said curtly.

'I've to be with my mother, Master,' I replied in the same tone.

'All day?'

'She's my mother!'

'Fine, then, be a mama's puppy.' And he hung up on me.

I felt hot near my ears. I wanted to fling the phone on the wall and watch it shatter into pieces. If it wasn't for the fear of my father's wrath, I probably would have done it. Still, I slammed the receiver as hard as I could. Mum was recovering. The injury had not affected her speech, sight or memory. She was eating. All was well. Things were looking up again, but Master's phone call ruined my morning.

'Master called,' I told mother dejectedly at the hospital and narrated the entire conversation verbatim.

'But Master is right, Vasu,' she said while fixing the collar of my shirt. 'There's no need for you to hang around the whole day.'

'Try this mango pickle, papa,' a plump lad of Varun's age said enthusiastically. 'It's mind-blowing.' Next to mum was a man who had had coronary bypass surgery. Every day, at least twenty people visited him and brought along tiffin boxes full of food. The whole room would smell of turmeric, pickles and what not.

I looked at mum again.

'But who will take care of you then?' I said angrily.

'Your father is here. The doctors are here. Mira has taken days off.'

'I also want to be here!'

'No, Banwari Lal!' the patient on the next bed insisted. 'I can't have jalebis even if they are made in pure desi ghee.'

'One jalebi is like a drop in a bucket, papa,' the son insisted. 'You won't even know where it went in your big tummy.'

They were rowdy and noisy. Their pickles and jalebis kept intruding into my conversation. I looked at him angrily and he offered me a jalebi in response.

'One day I would like to see my Vasu as a world champion,' mum said. 'You will be speaking to journalists on TV, they'll jostle to pose their questions to you and some of them will click your pictures in a frenzy. You'll walk away briskly soon after speaking to them.'

I smiled.

'None of this would be possible without your master, Vasu.'

'But he's so hard sometimes.'

'He's only saying it for your own good.'

'Do I just leave you here and push some pieces on a wooden board?'

'Okay, don't be upset! I'll have one jalebi,' the patient said. 'No! No pakora at all!'

'Will you please be quiet?' I got up and yelled. 'This is a hospital!'

'Calm down, Vasu.' Mum tugged at my arm.

'Why is he so mad, behenji?' the patient asked my mother. 'It's a short life.' He looked at me. 'Eat and be merry,' he said, putting the last jalebi in his mouth and then asked his son to quickly pack everything up as the doctor would be doing his rounds soon.

'You know, Vasu,' mother said, 'no one can make us understand anything if we choose not to. I know that you know what Master really meant.'

I kept quiet. There was some rust on the hinges of her bed.

It'll be nice if they had wooden beds in hospitals. Wonder why they don't.

'Besides you, I have your father, Mira and Varun, but Master only has you,' she added. 'Don't judge him for what he says, see him for what he does.'

The doctor came on a round. It was time to change her dressing too.

Trriiiinnng. I stood outside Master's home.

Trriiiiiiiinnnnng. I buzzed again.

As always, he opened the door a bit, looked out and then opened it fully. I latched the door behind me.

He opened two bottles of cola. Then he quietly spread the chess mat, made no mention of our phone conversation, didn't ask about mother, but simply gesticulated that I should set the chess clock. We played and, as usual, I lost. I'd already lost more than two thousand games against him and drawn a few. It had become a way of life. I always began with the assumption that I would lose. I tried to play smart, clever and fancy, but it would amount to nothing.

'Do you know the number of permutations possible in chess?' he asked at the end of a game.

'I heard it's more than the drops in the ocean.'

'It's 2.5×10^{18},' he said. 'You can't examine every single drop, Vasu. You can't observe all the waves.'

I kind of knew where he was going with this, but I couldn't be sure. You just couldn't tell whether he was deflecting, distracting or directing – all of it intentionally.

'Master the basics,' he added. 'Know when to float, versus when to swim or steer.' He coughed. 'How will you play in the tournament?'

Today, he was coughing more than usual.

'Why don't we go see a doctor?' I asked.

'That's not the answer to my question.'

'No!' I protested. 'I'm not listening to you any more. You must take proper medication.'

'Shut up, Vasu.' There was a coldness in his voice.

'Why are you always so mad? You think the world owes you something?'

'You can't change the topic!'

'I *am* taking proper medicine!' he said.

'This is crazy!'

'Vasu!' he spoke angrily. 'I'll tell you when I need what. All right?'

We both kept quiet for a few seconds. I wasn't angry with him, just concerned. He got up, took a sip of his cough syrup, straight from the bottle as if it were cola.

'The body is a frail vessel,' he said. 'The season is changing. Nothing to worry about. So tell me, how will you play in the tournament?'

'As Spielmann said once, "Play the opening like a book, the middle game like a magician, and the endgame like a machine",' I replied calmly.

'Imitation is good, but originality is better,' he said. 'Your mojo is in your own style.'

After mother's accident, I'd forgotten how much I'd enjoyed Master's nuggets of wisdom. Like a sculptor chiselling away one blow at a time, his pearls of insight always gave me something more to reflect on and admire.

'Who are you, Master?'

'What do you mean?'

'I saw how Dr D'Souza stood up in attention when you entered his cabin.'

In over a year that I'd know him, he had never shared anything about his background. Other than one old black-and-white picture of a lady, there was nothing that spoke of his association with any other human being at all. I didn't even know if that lady was his mother, wife, daughter, or someone else. I had asked him once out of curiosity, but he had only replied with a stern look.

The milkman, maid and postman – except for them. I never heard anyone else knock on his door. No one was ever invited;

no one dropped by. All this when he lived in the middle of a town bustling with people. Did they even know that a great player lived among them? I had tried to find some evidence of him playing in tournaments in the past. Without success.

Other than his story of the game against Kartik Mahadevan, he never gave away any hint. There were no mementos or trophies on the shelves. Would an amateur have a huge bookcase full of chess books in the living room, and another one in the bedroom?

With what had unfolded recently at the hospital, I thought he might give me a glimpse into his life. That he might just share something.

'It's not important, Vasu. Let's focus on what you are here for.'

'But I want to know. Please.'

'You will. When the right time comes.'

That was the end of the conversation.

The rest of the week went in reflecting on how grandmasters handled their pawns. Master's cough continued to bother me. It didn't subside at all. But that did not deter him. He would just not take rest though I insisted a few times. He remained eager and alert as ever. Much like a vulture flying several hundred feet up in the air spots even the most well-camouflaged mouse, Master was very good at spotting mating attacks.

In the midst of a heated game when attack seemed the best choice, a grandmaster would often move a harmless pawn. It rarely made sense to me, but it always sat well with the master.

He would go to great lengths to explain the rationale behind such moves and their implications. I would resolve to play like one of the grandmasters, but no matter what I decided, I would still lose the next game to him. The fights were getting better and I was drawing against him more often; yet, victory remained elusive.

It was a Sunday evening like any other. A boisterous group of children were playing cricket on the street. The neighbour's loud TV declared that the weekly movie was being televised. We were focusing on an intense game of chess that was well into its third hour. Twice we had had extension of time. Master wanted to play not rapid or blitz, but a full tournament-style game.

'Checkmate!'

With his head down, he continued to stare at the board for a few minutes and then raised his eyes to look at me. It wasn't the master who had said 'checkmate'. So many times I had imagined that moment. I thought I would jump up in exhilaration, do a little twist and jiggle my hips. But I think his dullness was rubbing off on me because all I did was announce it softly, though with a triumphant feeling.

Master sat there, smiling. He was looking at me fixedly, with a sense of fierce pride.

'Vasu,' he beamed, 'you are ready!'

I picked up my cola in Master's style today, indifferent and assured. I had a quiet sip and put it down. Of course, this was only to camouflage my real feelings. I was overwhelmed.

I offered to play one more game but he needed to rest, he said. I had an inkling that he wasn't telling me the complete story. It wasn't just cough; it couldn't be. Every now and then, I would notice the syrups having been changed or strips of different tablets and capsules, but that was about it. Or maybe I was just being paranoid.

Mum was to be discharged the next day but I had to go to school. I still had to give the written apology to my drawing teacher, apply for leave so I could go to the tournament and, above all, see Rea. She would be waiting, I thought. I certainly was. How my heart raced at the thought of her. Rea was sitting where she had promised she would! It felt strange sitting next to a girl who had mocked me and then got me suspended. Only momentarily, though. Most girls in the class had their hair in plaits, but she was dazzling in a shoulder-length cut, her hair straightened. She had a wide forehead, large eyes, a pixie nose and pink lips.

'So? Did you miss me?'

'Did you?' I asked.

'Of course, I missed you every day,' she said excitedly. 'I wrote you a letter every day.' And she handed me a bunch of letters. Plus two chocolates.

But it wasn't the chocolate or letter that gave me the sizzles. It was the accidental touch of her hand when I took those from her. Or maybe it wasn't accidental. She had smiled. Her hands were soft, like freshly churned cream; that's all I could feel during that graze. I was too nervous to hold them.

I was self-conscious the whole time. *Am I looking all right?* Immediately after lunch, I felt that something was stuck in my teeth. *I hope it's not coriander.* I smiled without parting my lips until I had the opportunity to check in the mirror.

'My mother was in hospital the whole week,' I told her during the last period. 'She fell down and had a brain injury.'

'Oh my God!' She drew closer and clasped my hands.

Now that's a jackpot! You should have told her about mum in the morning, Vasu. How nice she smells. Like lavender.

I told her that mum was okay now and about how stressful the week had been. Her hands held mine the whole while.

It was Friday already, and she'd been getting me a little chocolate every day. She wrote beautiful letters to me, drawing hearts, kisses, flowers and butterflies. I too gave her a pocket chess set and wrote a long letter. I told her about my family and my master. She'd laughed so much when I told her about how Varun made me touch Muffin and had said that there were plenty of fish in the sea.

Yet, this only left me wanting more. All this talk had taken place in bits and pieces in class, stealing moments when teachers were busy. I wanted to sit down with her in a quiet corner and just talk without worrying about, let's say, getting suspended again.

For the next week and a half I would be away at the tournament. So I had to speak to her.

'Can you see me in the canteen after school?'

'Sorry, Vasu, I can't. My school bus leaves just a few minutes after the final bell.'

'Oh.'

'But the last period is free today,' she said. 'We can meet in the library or the school ground, near the water cooler.'

'Not the library,' I whispered.

'The cooler, then.'

For the rest of the day, I doodled hearts and various chess pieces in her notebook. Most notably, I drew the king and the queen and wrote her name under the queen. She beamed at me. The last period came after a long wait.

We sat under the shade. She began talking about her family.

'There's nothing glamorous about my family,' she said. 'I'm telling you upfront, Vasu.'

'How does that even matter?'

'My father owns a provision store,' she said.

Aha! That's where all the chocolates have been coming from!

'And at the back, my mother runs a small salon,' she continued. 'My mother was once offered a job at the university, but with a business set-up at home, she's able to care for my brother better.'

Rea's younger brother was autistic. Things were always stressful at home, since her parents had a lot of expectations from her. Specially because she would be the sole guardian of her brother in their absence.

I looked at my watch. It was nearly the end of the period. Forty-five minutes had passed in a blink.

'The bell may go off any time,' I said. 'Give me your phone number.'

'We don't have a phone at home. Just one at the shop.'

'Can I have the shop phone number, then?'

'My parents are really conservative, Vasu. They'll kill me if they find out I'm talking to a guy.'

'Don't worry, I won't call.'

She wrote down her phone number and I gave her mine.

'I'm going for a tournament next week,' I said. 'I wish I could talk to you over the phone from there.'

'How long will you be gone?'

'About twelve days.'

'Twelve days!'

She went quiet, as if upset.

Oh, how I wanted to hug her. Yet, all I managed to do was squeeze my left hand with my right palm. I sat there like an anxious player wanting to make a move, except that he must wait because it was the opponent's turn.

'There's something I want to tell you, Vasu,' she said gravely. 'But I'm not sure if or when to tell you.'

'Say it.'

'I'm a little scared.'

'You are not fooling around with me, Rea,' I chuckled, 'are you?'

'No, Vasu.' Her face turned grave. 'It's a serious matter.'

'Okay then, shoot. I can take it.'

'I don't know how to put this, Vasu,' she said hesitatingly. 'But I was—'

And the bell rang – long and loud – as if it were the end of time.

'You were what?'

'Not this time,' she said as she got up. 'I'll tell you some other day.'

'But I'm going away!'

'Yes, I'll tell you later.'

'Tell me now, Rea!' I cried. 'It's not fair!'

'My bus will leave any time.' She got up hurriedly and left. I sat there, intrigued. She swiftly took a few steps back, bent down, gave me a peck on my cheek and ran away.

'Win me the trophy, Vasu,' she hollered.

I walked slowly to the parking stand, making a million guesses, churning my thoughts regarding what Rea wanted to tell me, but that's all they were – guesses. Yet, somehow, I felt I had found my charm, my mojo in her.

9

MY BEST MOVE

'PLAY LIKE YOU'VE nothing to lose, Vasu,' Master said. 'Besides, it's true as well,' he laughed, 'you've got nothing to lose.'

'There's a small problem, Master,' I said. 'Dad may not get another week's leave since he just took time off due to mum's accident.' (Yes, an accident. I was too ashamed to give Master the details of the accident or admit the extent of my dad's involvement in the affair.)

'I was wondering if you could accompany me.'

'Vasu,' he said, 'I'll never accompany you to any tournament.'

'But Bangalore is a two-day train ride,' I pleaded. 'Dad won't allow me to travel alone.'

'Skip the tournament, then,' he said without even glancing at me.

'Skip it?' My ears burned. A surge of anger rushed through my body. Oh, how I controlled myself from kicking the table and slamming the bottle of cola on the floor. *Skip it?* 'Only last week you got mad at me for missing my practice, saying I had to play in this tournament.'

'I cannot accompany you,' he said again, calmly.

'But why?' My voice was getting louder.

'I can't tell you,' he said in his annoying monotone.

If I could, I would have smashed the bulb and hurled the chess clock at his vintage book case, shattering its glass, and for once see him lose his composure and see him act like a human being.

'That's ridiculous!'

'Stop yelling or get out of here.' He said it so easily, as if announcing a checkmate.

'Fine!' I picked my bag and stormed out of his home, banging the door shut as hard as I could.

This was certainly not how I had imagined going to my first rated tournament. The fee was already paid, the tickets and accommodation already booked. All I wanted was for my heartless teacher to join me. I didn't think it was too much to ask for. Dad was still at work, waiting for my call. I informed him that Master had refused.

'Don't worry, son,' he said. 'I'll speak to my boss.'

I would have skipped the tournament but the fee, travel and accommodation bookings were roughly equivalent to a whole month's salary for my dad. We had already incurred the expense. Even though he had shown no sign of worry, I knew I wasn't born to Dhirubhai Ambani. It wouldn't take Sherlock Holmes to figure out that dad only had a handful of shirts and trousers he had been wearing for years. Once a year, on Diwali, mother would go out and buy clothes for him. And the first prize in the tournament was eight thousand rupees.

Master or no master, I'm not going to waste my parents' money. I'll play.

Forty-eight long and tiresome hours in the train felt even longer because of a family sitting next to us with two kids. I was no stranger to noise; Varun was the noisy one at home. The real challenge was posed by peanuts. The family kept eating and throwing the shells right where we sat. It was hard to even go to the lavatory without stepping on the litter. Dad paid the sweeper twice to get it cleaned.

Every time I looked at them in an attempt to shame them into civility, they would tell me to teach their kids chess. Four times the kids spilled tea and, once, a whole bottle of water. They would hang from the upper berth, dangling their arms and legs right in our faces, jumping from one berth to the other like baby monkeys. Whenever they fought and cried and raised hell, which was roughly once every five minutes, the parents would give them something to eat.

They should be in a zoo!

If Varun and I ever dared fight like that in front of dad, he would probably have hung us upside down from the ceiling fan. And then turned it on. The hospitable mother of the two baby monkeys offered us peanuts for the umpteenth time and we eventually gave in. I was forced to choose between eating peanuts and teaching chess to the monkey brigade. I went with the peanuts.

Finally, we got off at Bangalore and reached the venue. It was a huge college campus turned into a chess venue. Sprawling lush green lawns, neatly trimmed hedges and a variety of flowers covered the periphery of the campus. There were not twenty, forty or fifty but all of two hundred participants who had flocked from all over the country. Some were sitting alone and practising, many were playing against each other.

I saw the registration list. It was unnerving, to say the least. I could imagine finishing the tournament exactly where I started – at the bottom of the list. There were twenty FIDE masters, ten international masters and three grandmasters. Some of the Indian heavyweights I used to read about in chess magazines roamed the lawns majestically. I took autographs from all three grandmasters. It was all very exciting. Except about ten participants, including myself, everyone was rated. Some were even older than my dad.

Though nervous, I was also thrilled to be part of a tournament with real GMs and Masters. Five days of just chess, chess and more chess, against the best. I had quite an opening and won many casual games against other players. This boosted my confidence, perhaps a bit too much, because it clouded my caution. But after losing the first two games, one of which was against an unrated player, I came back to my senses really fast. I drew the next one and won the last game of the day. My ranking at the end of day one was 150.

The competition got tougher on the second day as I was playing against opponents who had won a similar number of games the first day. Yet, Master's wisdom stood by my side like a guardian angel. I chose unconventional responses against known players and stuck to the basics in my moves. The strategy worked and I managed to win two out of four games on day two, losing the other two. My score was 3.5/8 at the end of day two. This was a very good score. I was in the top thirty now and it felt damn good to see my name in the first pairing sheet.

Day three, however, was a different ball game as I desperately scrambled for a draw even as I lost three good games. Absolutely no strategy worked. All of a sudden, my ranking dropped to seventy-eight. *This is crazy.* One bad day and I slid down like a skier from a high mountain. I tried an unconventional opening in my fourth game but it backfired and I lost the game in under thirty moves. *Hell, Master should have been here to guide me.* Soon, I was missing home. Dad was no good at lifting my morale.

I needed a lot more affection than a 'you win some, you lose some, Vasu.'

I hadn't come here to lose. I felt bad for myself but worse for my dad. He would just sit quietly and wait all day. It was no fun for him, for he didn't know chess at all. He would be waiting outside the room to see me as soon as I finished my game. More than losing, it was painful to tell him that I had lost – to see him shrug his wide shoulders and smile that quiet smile.

My head was hurting from feeling low and thinking more than I could handle. It felt like my brain would just pop out of my skull. 'I'll see you in the room, dad,' I said. 'I just want to take a stroll.'

'Don't go too far,' he warned. 'It's a new city.'

I nodded and agreed to meet him for dinner an hour later. I wanted to talk to someone – there was just one voice that would make everything all right, I felt. I opened the slip and stared at the number. I wasn't sure if I should call. *What the heck?* I walked into the phone booth and dialled the number.

'Hello,' the voice on the other end said.

'H ... he ...' I cleared my throat. 'Hello.'

'Yes, who's this?'

Really? Could someone who sounded like a street hawker from Akbar's time be the father of such a pretty girl? My heart was thumping and I felt itchy on my head. Even though I had dialled, I didn't know what to say to Rea's dad.

'How can I help you?' he asked.

Give the phone to your daughter.

I just put the phone down, feeling washed out. I called again after a few minutes.

'Hello.' The voice was louder this time.

My heart was wrestling to emerge from my chest. Again. Words would only end up as spit I would swallow.

'Hello?' he said. 'Who's this?'

'Rea Verma Provision Store?' I managed to blurt out a name, based on Rea's surname.

'No,' he said. 'It's Rea's Modern Mart.'

Of course!

'Who's this?' he asked again.

'I wanted to order some stuff.'

'Sure, sir.' The voice turned very polite. 'If your order is more than Rs 100, we'll do free home delivery.'

'Do you have Dairy Milk?'

'No dairy products here, sir.'

'Not milk, Dairy Milk, the chocolate?'

'Oh, sorry,' he said. 'Yes, we do.'

'I require thirty Dairy Milk chocolates, seven kilograms of corn flour, five kilograms of sugar, three kilograms of almonds, three kilograms—'

'Papa?' It was Rea's voice in the background.

Oh thank you, God. Thank you.

'Mum—'

'What papa?' he said to her.

'Excuse me?'

'Sorry, sir,' he said. 'Someone was here.'

'Mum's calling you,' Rea said in the background.

'I'm taking a customer's order,' he said to Rea. 'Stay here and help me pack it.'

You are here, Rea! Take the phone from your dad! Make my day!

'Yes sir,' he said. 'Three kilograms of what?'

'Rea.'

'Sorry?'

'Rea ... real ... real ghee, I mean.'

'We only sell real stuff, sir,' he said emphatically. 'Absolutely no adulteration.'

'Actually, it's my sister's sixteenth birthday,' I said. 'I wanted some gift ideas other than chocolates, for her friends. You won't happen to know someone her age, would you?'

'Why not, sir, my daughter can help you.'

I heard him say to Rea that it was a sizeable order and that the customer needed some help in selecting items for his sister's sixteenth birthday.

'I've nothing to suggest.' I could hear Rea tell her dad.

'Rea!' he said curtly. 'Speak to this gentleman.'

Sir, there's this thing called a mouthpiece. It's not a crime to put your hand on it while you talk to the other person.

'Hello.'

Ah! I felt a minor jolt, as if electricity passed through me in slow motion.

'Rea!' I squealed.

'Oh my God, Va ... very good, sir, very good,' she said.

'What happened?' her dad asked. 'Don't show so much eagerness even if it's a big order.'

'Mum said she wanted to see you urgently. I'll take the order.'

'Gone!' she whispered. 'Papa's gone. Vasu! You called!'

I told her about the argument with Master, not winning too many games, and how I'd been feeling low and dejected.

'I'm feeling lost, Rea. I don't know if I can do this ... this tournament.'

'Why don't you call your master?'

'After that argument?'

'Vasu,' she said firmly, 'he's your teacher. Call him.'

'No way!'

'Please do, Vasu. Do it for my sake. I want you to win.'

'Rea?' her dad said. 'Is the order complete?'

'Order? Umm ... yeah ... no ... I mean ... he was ... the phone got disconnected.'

'Put it down, then,' he shouted. 'How will he call back otherwise?'

'I love you,' she mumbled almost inaudibly.

Beeeeeep ...

My head was not hurting any longer. I was feeling confident again. Hunger was tugging at my tummy. Rea's voice was still running through me like blood through my veins. I desperately wanted to just hold her hand and hug her right at this moment. The whole conversation was playing back in my head.

I'm not going to call Master. If he doesn't need me, I don't need him either.

I met dad for dinner. He was surprised to see me cheerful. I was gorging on food like there was no tomorrow. He must have thought I got a dose of wisdom or something from the master.

'Did you speak to your master by any chance?'

'No.'

'You look rather happy after you got back from your walk.'

I just shrugged and carried on with my meal.

'We can call him from our room,' he offered.

I just shook my head.

We went back to our room, I practised some more and formulated my strategy for the next day. I knew how I would open with white but I still was bit unsure how should I play with black.

I'll figure something out, but I'm not going to call my master. Let him also wonder how am I faring in the tournament.

I went to bed with my thoughts jumping from Rea to mother,

from chess to Muffin, from Varun to Mira, and sometimes from Master to dad.

'Not just a grandmaster,' a soft voice whispered in my ears, 'I want to make you a world champion.'

'You've come, Master,' I exclaimed. 'You said you wouldn't join me.'

Master said nothing more. He was coughing. I waited for a little while.

He stood there quietly, looking at me unblinkingly. He was smiling.

'Don't leave me, Vasu,' he said. 'You're all I have.'

'Why did you throw me out?' I protested. 'You'd promised to never do that.'

'I'm an old man, son,' he said. 'I'm tired of living.'

I felt helpless. I wanted to make him feel all right and see him laugh. I lunged at him with an overwhelming need to hug him tight and wipe his tears. But he took a few steps back. Again, I stepped forward; again, he moved back.

'Why can't I reach you, Master?' I asked, scared. Stretching my arms out, I moved towards him.

Master's clothes turned white and light emitted from him. He began walking away from me, in the air, as if moonwalking.

'Don't leave me. Master!' I screamed. 'Master!' I called out. 'Where are you going?'

'Vasu, son? Vasu? Are you all right?' I opened my eyes to find my dad leaning over me.

'I just had a nightmare, dad. I want to call Master.'

'It's two in the night, Vasu! We'll call him in the morning.'

'No, dad, I must call him now!'

'Vasu, he's an old man, it's not right to trouble him like this.'

Old man? Yes, that's what Master said as well.

For the first time, I realized that Master was indeed an old man and that one day, he would no longer be there. I felt dizzy. What would I do without him? Chess seemed meaningless without my master. If it was just me, chess would be simply a game. He made it come alive. It was my master more than anyone else who I wanted to please by winning my games.

I don't know how long it took, but I fell asleep again and the morning alarm woke me up. I rushed through my breakfast and went straight to the phone booth.

Tring ... tring. Tring ... tring. Tring ... tring. Tring ... tring.

His phone continued ringing. I felt as if my heart had slipped out of its place. I dialled again. It rang again. Even if something terrible had happened, the milkman would be there soon, he would knock and suspect something. The maid would also come around mid-day. She would wonder, and hopefully alert the neighbours. I rang once again.

Tring ... tring. Tring ... tring. Tring ... tring.

I'll call Varun and ask him to reach Master's place and break open the door.

'Hello.'

'Varun, sorry, I mean Master,' I said. 'Where were you?'

'I was here.'

'I tried calling you so many times!'

'I was in the washroom, Vasu!' he said softly. 'An old man needs his time and peace in the washroom.'

'I was worried.'

'So was I, Vasu. I called your home last night to find out if you'd reached safely.'

'I only won four out of twelve games. Drew two.'

'Not bad,' he said. 'It's your first tournament.'

'That's what dad says, but I want to do better!'

'There are still two days to go!'

'Yes, but I don't know what to do.'

'Go back to the basics,' he replied. 'No fancy moves, no thinking about numbers and points. Just the game. Before making—'

'I wish you were here!'

'—before making any move, ask yourself a simple question: "Is this my best move?"'

'You think I can win?'

'Vasu,' he said firmly. 'You know everything there is to know about the game. Play it in your own style.'

'I'm just scared.'

'Of what?'

'Of losing.'

'Losing what?'

'The tournament!'

'You are not there to win the tournament. You are there to show the world that you know how to play the game. Better than them. One move at a time.'

One move at a time. This insight hit me like lightning on a lone tree in a vast prairie. *I don't have to think about points and winnings and prize money. I just have to play a lot of good moves.*

After losing the first game on the fourth day, I went on to win the remaining three. With a score of 7/16, my ranking shot up and I was on number nineteen. We called home from our room. Mother worried about how I was holding up under all that stress. Varun was having a blast, he told me. In dad's absence, he woke up late in the mornings and got back home late in the evenings. Mira was busy with her painting as usual. Though she didn't play chess, she showed the most interest over the phone to know how was I doing in my tournament, what was it like, whether I was enjoying the whole thing.

On the fifth and the final day, I played most strategically. I went in with the mind-set that I would play closed games with extreme patience. Closed games lead to tense and tight situations in the middle of the board. It requires complete mastery over tactical play if one is to have any chance in closed games. I had already paid the price of impatience and overconfidence. The strategy really paid off and I went on to win all four games on the final day. My final score stood at a commendable 11/20.

It wasn't a stellar performance but I had wrapped up much better than I had hoped for in the first three days of the tournament. The first place was shared by two grandmasters, the second one was secured by a grandmaster as well. The third place was taken by a new unrated player. No, it wasn't me. Vasu Bhatt showed up fourth on the list. The prize money was peanuts for the player ranking fourth, but it wasn't the prize money that was the real reward for me. It was the rating. Yes, I had become a rated player. Master sounded pleased to hear that over the phone.

I had secured two wins against two different IMs and one against a GM. IM stands for International Master, a rated player with a rating of or higher than 2400. It felt funny reporting the result at the bench with the same GM whose autograph I had sought just four days back. It was an awesome feeling to be in the big league.

Those victories had given me a solid start. As a result, my rating by FIDE, Fédération Internationale des Échecs, also known as the World Chess Federation, opened very high. An Elo rating of 1948. This might sound like the year of Mahatma Gandhi's assassination but it was actually a very good thing (the rating). 1948 was something to celebrate, because if I continued this way, with a rating of 2400, I could be an IM in one year.

Heck, I could even be a GM. All I needed to attain the title of GM was a rating of more than 2500, and fulfil some other criteria. It felt surreal that I was so close to the titles that had once looked as far as the twinkling stars in an unknown universe.

I went to see Master as soon as I got home. He opened the door at the first bell. I bowed down to touch his feet. Today I was feeling more reverent because his single phone call had given me hope and confidence at the end of day three.

No congratulations. That's not how he worked. The first thing he said was, 'Did you annotate your games?'

'All but the drawn.'

'Always annotate all games,' he said. 'It is how we go back into your head to know you better. And the more you know yourself, the better you become at everything you do.'

He walked to the fridge, got two bottles and came back to sit in the rocking chair that lay diagonally to where I sat. He always sat in the rocking chair except when we were playing a game of chess. Then he would sit in the couch opposite mine.

Tssss ... He handed me the bottle of cola. The bottle opener was always on the side table next to his chair. A small timepiece, the phone, a notepad with a pen and a bottle opener occupied that side table, always.

Tssss... That sound of the bottle opening would always make me thirsty.

He mercilessly analysed my games over the next four hours. His cough was much better; he actually didn't cough even once. Out of all the games I lost, one stood out in particular. It was a clear case of reckless moves. I'd sacrificed my knight even though there was no mating attack in sight. My annotation read that

I had done it in the hope that my opponent would move his bishop thereafter; he simply started exchanging pieces.

'What were you thinking?' Master said, a bit annoyed.

'You won't be mad?'

'Go on.'

'This was my first game and he was an unrated player too. He looked so shabby and distracted, so unlike a chess player, that I never thought he had any chance against me. He actually went on to win one game after the other and eventually came third in the tournament.'

Master chuckled.

'I don't blame you, Vasu,' he said. 'It can happen. It happened to me many years ago...'

I HAD ALREADY won a few prestigious tournaments. I was sitting in a park once. With a chess book in my hand, I was playing practice games.

A young girl, hardly seven years old, was walking with a lady, probably her mother. They came and stood next to me. I paid no attention at first, but some ten minutes later, they were still standing there. It was a bit annoying to have them hovering around. Yet, I ignored them, until the older lady said, 'Can the little one have a game with you?'

'Excuse me?' I exclaimed.

I looked at the girl as I uttered those words. Most unusually, though, I felt that those hazel eyes in her innocent face were laughing at me, challenging me. It made me uncomfortable. To be invited to play against someone who had just graduated out of toddlerhood when I was a rated player – well, it hurt my ego big time. Really, I thought the mother should just go home and give her a doll to play with.

I could not say no, though, for it would have been impolite. After all, it was not about winning or losing with the little one. It was just meant to give her a game.

The little girl sat across me and I set up the board.

'I'll play without my queen,' I said. 'You'll enjoy more that way and, who knows, you may even beat me!' I said, smiling benignly.

'Thank you, but that won't be necessary,' she said gravely. 'Let's play an equal game.'

'All right, doll.' The game would be over before you count to twenty, I thought. 'You take white,' I said, maintaining my fake smile.

'Okay.' She shrugged her tiny shoulders in her pink outfit. Extending her hand for the customary handshake, she said, 'Good luck.'

She opened with the king's knight, which was a bit too big for her little hands. It looked very cute. I couldn't help but grin. I responded with king's pawn. Her next move was to move the rook's pawn to its full two steps. That moment I knew I was playing against an absolute beginner. I was already imagining giving her some tips to improve her moves at the end of the game and where all she went wrong. Over the next fifteen moves, I was two pawns down with a significantly weaker position. Even a layman could tell that all my pieces were on the defence. Her highly unconventional moves had taken me by complete surprise. Another twenty moves, and the game was over.

I lost. I wished there were a well around so I could jump right in. I'd mistaken my experience for wisdom. I tried my best to sound normal when I said, 'You play really well. I didn't think you had a chance.'

'Why? I had as much a chance of winning as you, sir,' she replied.

'Let's play another game,' I offered.

'Thank you, but I've had my win for the day,' she said and got up and left.

The girl and her mother walked away swiftly. After they disappeared from my sight, I, as if woken up from a dream, ran looking for them leaving my book and my chess board behind. They were nowhere to be found. It was a big open park. Where could they have gone in such a short span, I thought. Twenty minutes later I returned after a vain search. I sat there zapped and dazed. I learnt the biggest lesson of my life. Never judge your opponent: not from their appearance, manners, way of talking, words ... from nothing. Not even from their game. Just don't judge them.

'COULD YOU EVER trace them?' I cut him off.

'No, Vasu,' he said. 'The little girl must be a prodigy or something, and her mother knew from the outset that I'd be defeated at her tiny hands. That clever duo! You see, Vasu, human intelligence is beyond age and experience. There is no better example than chess to prove it, where there are kids younger than you holding the title of GM.

'The truth is, Vasu, the tournament was yours to take home, and instead of fourth you could have stood first. Had you begun it with the same rigour you showed on the fourth and fifth day, you would have easily been sitting here with the trophy. As Rudyard Kipling said:

If you can fill the unforgiving minute,
With sixty seconds' worth of distance run,
Yours is the Earth and everything that's in it

'If you had poured in every game, everything that you knew, every strategy, every tactic you had learnt, you'd have emerged at the top, a winner,' Master said.

How easy he made it sound! If I could win on the last day, I could win on the first too. If I had been less full of myself, maybe ... but perhaps it was a good thing that I didn't go on to win the tournament. Success probably would have gone to my head. I might even have started to believe that I had outgrown my master.

Truth be told, chess was important in my life because of him. It may not have been the best move, but sometimes it's not about the best move at all. It's just about a fulfilling, wholesome move. Sometimes, the best way is to enjoy the journey with your co-traveller than rushing to the destination. For the joy of seeking is more exhilarating than attaining what's sought.

10

THE RIGHT TO DREAM

'WHAT DID YOU want to tell me the other day, Rea?' I said as soon as I met her. Even before asking how she was doing and the rest of that formality.

'It's a beautiful sunny day, isn't it?'

'Rea.'

'Let's talk about your tournament,' she said.

'No!' I insisted. 'First you tell me.'

'Can we not talk about this some other time?'

'Now! Please.'

'Vasu,' she said. 'I fear that you'll start hating me.'

'The suspense is killing me, Rea!'

'Will you keep it to yourself?'

'Just say it!'

'Okay, Vasu,' she said gravely. 'Don't hate me afterwards.'

I became nervous, as if I was about to play against a grandmaster. I had no clue what her next move would be. The longer the silence stretched, the more tense I got. Rea lowered her head. Her hands absent-mindedly played with the hem of her skirt that ended right below her bony knees. She fumbled with her words a couple of times, let out a deep sigh and then looked me straight in the eye.

'I'm an adopted child.'

'What?'

Before I could say more, she continued, 'The matron at the orphanage said that I was found abandoned outside a tobacco shop, a small stall. It was on Shivaratri. A few metres away, to the right of the stall, was a mosque where the muezzin was calling out azan from the minaret. And to the left, at about an equal distance, was a Shiva temple where they were chanting eulogies to Shiva. My adoptive mother, sometimes in a fit of rage, is quick to remind me that they don't even know if it's Hindu or Muslim blood running in my veins. I'm an outcast. I've no identity of my own—'

'Oh, Rea—'

'Let me finish, Vasu,' she continued in a sombre tone. 'Mama says that they didn't adopt me because they wanted a daughter. They did it because they wanted someone who could take care of their autistic son. Papa, however, disagrees with mama and never fails to express his love for me. Whether it's buying new shoes, clothes, sending me away on school camps, or giving me a chocolate every day, he has always gone beyond his means to care for me. And I do love Rahul. He's the sweetest brother in the world. He's a real brother to me even though I am not related to him by birth. I spent the first seven years of my life in an orphanage.'

She vividly remembered her last three years at the orphanage. People would often donate blankets and socks in winter, but they were taken away from them soon after the donor left. She couldn't understand why then, but had now figured out that the custodians would sell it in the market and embezzle the money. They used to look forward to Holi and Diwali because some generous patrons would come and distribute sweets to them.

These were the only times that the kids would know what the taste of sweets and candies felt like.

She didn't go to bed hungry, she said, but never on a full tummy either. It was just a way of life at the orphanage – shabbiness, hunger, sadness gnawing at you all the time. There were elders to look after the children, some even kind, but most of them didn't care if the kids were sad or happy, full or hungry, clean or dirty, as long as they seemed healthy and happy enough for the donors to fawn over them and make large donations.

I heard her tale in shock and horror. I couldn't believe this tender, dainty girl, my princess, had once been little more than a ragged beggar or a street child.

But most of all, my blood boiled at how Rea's adoptive mother taunted her. For a moment I found myself philosophizing about what the better choice was – to have a mother who would demean you but feed you, or to live in an orphanage.

'This is terrible, Rea,' I said. 'I'm sorry for everything you went through.'

She was silent.

'Your mother is so cruel!'

'No, Vasu,' she turned towards me and said without any emotion in her eyes. 'I remember feeling hungry and crying for food at the orphanage and getting severely beaten in return. At least my parents don't beat me. I don't go to bed hungry. Mama is hard sometimes, but papa really protects and loves me. He lets me take chocolates, cold drink and candies from the shop. It was my dream to have parents. And no matter what, they *are* my parents, Vasu.'

I got up somewhat awkwardly and gave Rea a tight hug. I wanted to hold her forever.

'How could you even think that I would hate you for this,

Rea? I'm in love with you all over again. More than ever. I'll always keep you safe.'

How my heart melted as she nudged closer, only slightly, but I felt that she believed that I'd be there for her. And, by God, I would. I decided right that moment.

A few seconds passed and we stayed like that. It was the sweetest embrace in the world. She smelled like rose, but it wasn't just rose. There was some other underlying note of a different fragrance, I couldn't really tell.

'Did you help your mum in the kitchen today?'

'How do you know?' she exclaimed.

'Because I smell ginger and turmeric,' I joked.

She immediately moved back.

Oh you dumb idiot! Happy now?

'I must smell awful!' she said.

I spent the next ten minutes trying to convince her that I was only joking, but she remained unhappy.

Not just chess, Vasu, you need lessons in how to keep your girlfriend happy, and when to keep your mouth shut.

With each passing day, I only loved her more. In a way, she was like chess, only much more unpredictable. Every time I thought I had her figured out, she would take me completely by surprise. I had never enjoyed being in school as much as I did now. I would look forward to getting up in the morning and reaching my classroom. Two years sped by. But much had happened, and in a big way. I had won eight major tournaments in the last two years. Twice I had been interviewed by *ChessMate*, India's only chess magazine. They even printed my picture, a tiny black-and-white one, in which I was barely recognizable. Varun teased me about it, drew a moustache on it and stuck it on our dresser. 'Munshiji wanted,' he wrote underneath.

I even won a 'Student of the Year' award at school. They featured me in the annual school magazine. Mother had gone around and shown it to the neighbours and everyone else she could get a hold of, including our maid and the local scrap dealer. Regional and national newspapers had profiled me in the past two years, thankfully with better pictures.

IT WAS MY seventeenth birthday that day, but that's not why it was a special day. It was because I had managed to pass my Class XII examination. Actually, a more truthful way to put it would be that, somehow, I had managed to not fail. I had no desire for further studies. Besides, joining a regular college was out of question because my chess regime demanded travel and time. At dad's insistence, I got admission in Bachelor of Arts by distance education. I chose to specialize in philosophy. At least a basic university degree was necessary, he said. He would not let me play chess if I completely ignored my education. I wasn't happy about it, but he made sense and I couldn't argue.

To everyone's surprise, Varun had managed to gain admission in MBA at a prestigious institution. Given his less-than-commendable academic track record, all the girl-chasing and the boy-bashing, he had shocked all of us by clearing the entrance examination with great marks. Though dad was greatly relieved – because a job was almost certain upon graduation – he was equally stressed because he would have to arrange the finances. Varun's tuition fee, his hostel and living expenses, they were beyond what dad's salary could afford.

'Don't worry, papa,' Varun had said. 'I will give private tuitions and take care of my expenses.'

And he did that. That boisterous brother of mine had

suddenly grown up. Dad only had to pay his fee, which was substantial yet manageable. As soon as Varun moved out, it became very quiet, as if the soul of our home was gone. He was the talkative one, the liveliest of all of us. I would come home to a quiet room. No one was poking Muffin any more, and the other bed in my room was always unoccupied.

Sometimes I would shut the door and lie down on his bed. Munshiji, Munshiji ... would ring in my ears. How I missed him teasing me! I missed going on bike rides with him. I wanted to hit him with my pillow again. At times, it would become somewhat unbearable and I would call him and ask him to tell me about life in the hostel. On some days, he would be in his element and make my stomach hurt with laughter even on the phone; but on many days, he was quiet and introspective.

He was the only one in the family who knew about Rea and teased me about it incessantly. I told him that she also played some chess.

'Hmmm...' Varun said. 'Mating won't be easy, then. It may just be a stalemate sometimes.'

'Varun!'

'I hope your kids don't look like pawns, Munshiji,' he joked. 'Black or white!'

The first time I'd arranged for him to meet Rea, I requested him not to make fun of me in front of her.

'Trust me, Vasu,' he said. 'She'll fall head over heels for you after she meets me.'

He sat her down and told her my childhood stories – all inappropriate, in my opinion. He annoyed me in particular when he told her that since I was the youngest, I always got his used clothes. Varun had outgrown his shirts and shorts, whereas they were a bit too big for me. He went on to tell her that since

I had always been so thin, half the time my shorts would come down like the water level in the municipal tank – fast and furious.

'You won't believe, Rea,' Varun said, 'one hand of his was always holding his knickers, whether he was playing or running or even walking. He just wouldn't let go of it.'

Rea cupped her mouth with her hands and laughed.

'I mean, really,' Varun said, 'do you think anyone cares if a six-year-old is with or without shorts? Besides—'

'Varun!' I tried to stop him.

'—besides, until he was about five years old,' he added, 'he mostly ran around naked in the house.'

They laughed their heart out while I felt both shy and mad.

'But he's the genius in our family,' Varun finally said. 'We all love him the most. I don't know what all he does with the wooden chips all day, but—'

'Chess, Varun, they're not wooden chips!'

'—but, his master says that one day Vasu will be a world champion.'

'That day, Rea,' he said, 'I'll throw the biggest party.'

I felt all warm inside.

'Indeed, a grand party,' Varun added, 'will be the best use of his prize money.'

We burst into laughter. I felt both happy and sad. Varun was now in a different city, and I was very lonely without him.

Mira was twenty-five years old with a master's degree in anthropology and a stellar academic record. She had been a topper throughout. She got a job with the Department of Language and Arts. There were two vacancies and more than six hundred candidates. Rumour had it that many candidates were offering large sums of money to secure that job. The corrupt officers inside called it 'placement fee'. Mira had absolutely no chance because we just didn't have that kind of money. It was a painful fact that, despite her excellent score, she might still not get the job. More than angry, we were eager and desperate: it wasn't every day that we had a government opening in our small town.

I had mentioned it to Master, never expecting him to do anything about it. He had said nothing either. But then the next day, a call came from Mr Singh's office. He was the chairman of the department. They had confirmed Mira's job and an appointment letter was being dispatched by registered post, he said. Master wouldn't admit any hand in this. He was no less a mystery now than he was three years ago – but a mystery I couldn't imagine my life without.

Meanwhile, talks of Mira's marriage were going on at home. Our parents were busy looking for a suitable match for her. It was a stressful period because the groom had to be earning well, be a teetotaller and a Brahmin from a nuclear family. If this was not enough, the horoscopes had to match as well. Plus, we were strictly against dowry.

Sometimes everything would seem right, but the prospective groom would say that he wanted a girl who was a homemaker. On other occasions, they would say that they wanted a professional and not a government employee. For some, Mira was a bit short and for some her height was a little more than the groom's. And at other times, Mira would reject the proposal saying she couldn't see herself with someone who didn't earn more than her, or that she didn't want to marry a businessman or that the person must be at least as educated as her. Every other day, mother would run to the pandit to match horoscopes, but he was pickier than any mother-in-law in the world – he would always find something wrong with the match.

In some cases, the groom's parents would announce proudly that even though their son was on an official salary of just a few thousand rupees per month, there was plenty of 'other money and perks'. It was incredible to see how income from bribes and corruption was considered part of the package. Some would say softly that they didn't want anything in dowry but if my parents wanted to give furniture, jewellery, appliances, or a car, etc., to Mira, they would not object.

There were some good matches from non-Brahmin families, but our parents were, sadly, against it.

'We are broad-minded,' they would say, 'but, that doesn't mean we forego our traditions.'

And even if they were to relent, there was enormous pressure from our relatives to marry within the caste. At such times, I always thought of what would happen when Rea and I decided to be together for life.

There were weekly 'showings' of Mira and someone would either come to our home or she would be taken to a neutral location like a temple or a restaurant where the potential husband and Mira could steal a glance at each other. All this felt like a big joke, as if Mira was a cow being taken to the animal fair to be showcased to potential buyers. The poor girl was quiet through most of the ordeal.

'You are so lucky you are a guy,' Mira said to me once. 'If I could, I just wouldn't marry. I feel bad our parents have to go through all this. And for myself. I hate dressing up like a mannequin in a shop window, with a fake smile pasted on my face.'

'Soon your Mr Right will dig that smile, Mira,' I said to cheer her up, 'and whisk you away from us in no time.'

'Oh, Vasu,' she said irritably, 'it's not funny.'

Finally, after nearly ten months of frantic searching, matching and smiling, she found the love of her life, so to speak – Mohan Vasisht, an accountant who worked in the same department as her. The match was suggested by Ganju uncle whose wife's boss, a chartered account, was friends with Mohan. His parents said they wanted absolutely nothing in dowry. They just wanted to throw a big party, a nice reception, and have us foot the bill. How generous of them, especially when the guest list had *only* a few hundred people on it.

The situation had become a little tense, but eventually my parents thought that the match was too good to let go, so they agreed to the condition. Half of dad's provident fund was spent in funding the wedding. The other half in paying for Varun's tuition fee. Plus, chess wasn't cheap. Tournament fees, travelling to various locations, lodging, all required chips. On most occasions, I would recover the costs by winning the prize money, but the rest of the time, it really pinched to be asking dad for money.

After Mira's wedding, my parents were greatly relieved, for a major milestone had been achieved. Even though they stretched themselves financially, at least Mira was married to a good family. What they were little prepared for, however, was a ton of other expenses in the first year after the wedding. These were the first festivals.

On the first Holi, the first Diwali, the first karva-chauth, their first anniversary, Mohan's first birthday (as if he was just born), on everyone's birthday and anniversary in Mira's in-laws' family, they expected my parents to give them gifts and other 'tokens of love'. It was a New Year's day and Varun was there as well. Everyone was home, including Mira's in-laws.

'I feel really bad, Vasu,' she said. 'I don't like that our parents have to keep spending on hosting my in-laws.'

'If you won't tell them, Mira,' I said, 'they'll keep milking us.'

'You think I should open my mouth?'

'Why, haven't our parents made us strong enough to speak our mind?'

'What good is working for the Department of Language and Arts, Mira,' Varun said, 'if you can't artfully send the message across?'

'Artfully, huh?' she said. 'I'll speak to Mohan.'

'Now that's like a good girl!' Varun pulled her leg. 'Tell our lovely Mohanji to stop stealing butter like Krishna.'

'Mohan is a nice guy, Varun,' Mira retorted instantly.

'Tell him to be a good boy instead and buy whatever his parents need.'

Mira merely rolled her eyes but after that day she put her foot down, much to the chagrin of her in-laws, and forbade our parents from spending on gifts and hosting them during every small and big occasion in the calendar.

Time passed slowly after Mira's wedding. Varun graduated and got a job in the same city as his college. Two years of struggle and he was more serious and mature than ever before. Mira got busier with her new family. It would just be the four of us at home – our parents, Muffin and I. Dad's temples and sideburns had a lot of grey hair now. Fine lines had appeared on mother's face. Yet, there was no difference in the way I was treated at home. She worried about my diet vocally, and he about my career, but quietly.

At nineteen years of age – the year was 1989 – I looked forward to going to the biggest chess tournament of the time: the Linares International Chess Tournament in Spain. Started just a few years earlier, it was fast emerging as the Wimbledon of chess. We applied for a passport, but the officer wouldn't give it to me unless we gifted him a photograph of Mahatma Gandhi, the one that you find on a hundred rupee note. Dad said he would approach the officer's boss but remained firm about not paying anything as bribe.

I found the right opportunity to sneak in and quietly offered the man a junior Gandhi – fifty rupees. The passport was released within minutes.

Of course, I lied to dad that the officer relented seeing that I was going to represent our country at a chess tournament. I just wanted to have my passport and get my visa without any drama. Lying and bribing wasn't my style, but I couldn't afford a delay when I was going to play in my first overseas tournament. And while the tournament was important for me, I was well aware that funding it wouldn't be a breeze. Dad told me to focus on my game and not worry about finances. He had arrangements in place, he said.

I returned home from Master's one day to walk into a moment of uncomfortable silence. It wasn't the usual quiet. There was something strange about it even though I couldn't figure out what. Maybe it was because Duggal uncle, our family friend, who also happened to be the jeweller who had made all the gold jewellery for Mira's wedding, had come by himself. Whenever he visited our home all these years, he had always been accompanied by his wife.

They were having tea and Duggal uncle was carrying a bag. I sat down, curious, but Dad said that they required privacy for a while, and I went into my room. The visitor left after tea and mother was back in the kitchen preparing dinner. Dad came in to my room. He said he was proud of me that I would be playing in the Linares. He gave me a big lecture on how to stay away from strangers, keep my traveller's cheques and passport safe. Dad asked me to carry emergency numbers with full contact information in my wallet at all times.

'Tomorrow, we'll pay the tournament fee and book your tickets,' he said. 'We require those documents for the Spanish visa.'

'Why was Duggal uncle here?'

'He just stopped by for a cup of tea.'

'By himself?'

'Why not?'

'What are you not telling me, dad? What's wrong?'

'Vasu!' he said a bit gruffly. 'Don't read anything into the situation. There's nothing to tell.'

'I was concerned, that's all.'

'Don't think about the expenses, Vasu,' he said. 'We've got it covered.'

'But I didn't mention money!'

He brushed that aside and asked me to just focus on my practice and play the best I could. Then he went into the kitchen to help mother.

For the first time, I felt that perhaps I ought to have acquired a proper degree and got a proper job. I could have played chess part-time. Like Mira, I would have been financially independent too. Like Varun, I would have also got a job upon graduation.

I wouldn't be hovering around like a desperate bumblebee over a dry flower then. While most parents of their age were planning for life after retirement, my dad was still running from pillar to post, arranging funds for me.

This was the checkmate I hadn't seen coming at all.

The boat was midway now. There was no going back.

Other than it being my first – and solo – overseas trip, the prize money at Linares was a big attraction. The first position would give me enough to not only cover my expenses but have a decent financial buffer for the next two years. It would ease my parents' financial burdens too. This was my ticket to freedom. I dreamed on.

I would buy a saree for mum and a pendant for Rea from my winnings. But I also knew that I was counting my chickens before the hen and cock even got together. Linares would be harder than anything I'd ever played. There would be more than a hundred GMs there, and IMs by the dozens. Yet, I had the right to dream. Don't we all? Sometimes, that's the only beautiful thing about life – our dreams.

11

THE CHESS MISSILE

'CROWS ARE CAWING, Vasu,' mother had said when I was leaving for Linares. 'Let a few minutes pass now before you leave. It's an ill omen.'

'These dumb crows can't stop me from coming back a winner, mum,' I said, dragging my suitcase out of the house.

I clapped hard. A trio of crows perched on the terrace railing flew away frightened. I mooed loudly like a cow. My panicked mother cupped her mouth with both hands.

'That should cancel the omen now,' I said, making an innocent face.

Mother forcefully fed me a spoon of yoghurt and sugar. I felt its cool texture tingling the inside of my mouth. She told me to be cautious and not trust any stranger. But above all, she reminded me that I must only focus on chess and not worry about anything else.

'Don't be down when you lose a game or two,' she preached. 'Losses lead to victories for those who don't give up.'

The flight to Linares was a plain affair since, between boarding and disembarking, I didn't realize how time went by. I thought it would be a big deal but practice games and chess puzzles gobbled up my time. The plane landed safely at Linares. My luggage didn't.

I went from one corner of the airport to the other, and saw many suitcases indifferently going around in circles on luggage belts, all but mine. All my clothes were in the suitcase, but I wasn't too worried about them. A chess player can easily survive on one set of clothes, smell like fish, look unkempt and dishevelled, and still be considered a genius. But my chess set, clock and strategy sheets – those I needed. My little Bajrang Bali was in there too.

I spotted an airport official in a turban, a Sikh gentleman. Relieved, I ran towards him. The tall Sikh, however, greeted me not in Hindi or English but Spanish.

'Luggage problem,' I said in broken English, hoping that even if he didn't understand English, at least he would know some words.

'*De la* India?' he said.

I had no clue what he said but hearing the mention of India, I jumped with joy.

'Yes, yes, India, India!' I said.

He chuckled softly and spoke to me in Punjabi with a Spanish accent. I could understand most of it because Punjabi was quite similar to Hindi. He made a few calls and assured me that my luggage would be delivered at my hotel in the next two days. He even gave me his personal phone number and told me to contact him in case of any problems.

Two days to deliver my stuff? I regretted shooing the crows off our balcony. But were they done teaching me a lesson yet?

At the hotel, the first man I saw in the lobby was Andrei Kulikov, the chess missile. He was given that epithet for his merciless and annihilating attacks that left his opponents gasping for breath. Andrei never played to draw and always went for the kill. My hopes of winning the tournament disappeared upon seeing him.

He was sitting like a wax statue with a sort of Mona Lisa smile – I couldn't tell whether he was smiling or mad. Or maybe God had only given him a straight line by way of lips. Andrei's coach, a former world No. 1, sat opposite him. Two men, also in t-shirts bearing corporate logos, were scribbling something in notebooks. It was no secret that Andrei travelled with an entourage of his coach and two chess analysts at all times. They were his think-tank.

I nearly went closer to check him out personally, maybe even shake his hand, but my heart was thumping – what if he just shooed me away?

Every veteran in the chess world had predicted that he would be the next world champion. Andrei had an intimidating coldness about him. Not much was known about him apart from the ingenious attacks he had coined even in the most hopeless games. The famous Kulikov Bullet was named in his honour after he practically came back from the dead, checkmating the reigning world champion from a position that was as good as lost.

Regardless of his victories and fame, Kulikov was a private man. Journalists dreaded interviewing him; he was curt and unfriendly, almost hostile.

'It's beyond your peanut-sized brain,' he had said ending the last interview in one sentence when a reporter asked him about how he devised a strategy before every tournament.

A man of very few words, and fewer gestures, he often refused to shake hands with the opponent at the end of the game. Was it arrogance or a lack of social skills, or both? Andrei's impenetrable, expressionless mask of a face was discomforting, to say the least.

Make him lose to someone else, Bajrang Bali, so I don't have to face this monster.

I checked in and made a couple of quick calls to my parents and Rea. I kept the calls brief because I wanted to speak at length with my master. Unlike Andrei, I didn't have my coach with me to share my thoughts. At least, I could take heart by hearing his voice.

Master picked up the phone at the first ring.

'Master!' I screamed in both elation and anxiety. 'Guess whom I saw!'

'Umm ... Vasu,' he said, 'I was just stepping out.'

'I saw Andrei Kulikov. *The* Andrei Kulikov!'

'That's good, Vasu,' he said as if he hadn't heard me. 'I'm going to my village for a few days.'

'Oh. Can't you postpone the visit?'

'It's urgent.'

'How will I contact you?'

'I'll call you from there in the next couple of days.'

'Do you promise?' I reconfirmed. 'I must speak to you so I know how to fight against Andrei.'

'I will call you.'

'I hope it doesn't turn out like last time,' I continued. 'I must speak to you or I know I'll lose.'

'Vasu,' he said. 'Listen to your inner voice. I won't be there forever.'

'I don't know about forever, but this time I must have your guidance. Please.'

'I'll definitely try to call you, Vasu. Got to go.' And he hung up on me.

Try? Just a few sentences ago, he'd promised he would call me and now he said he would try.

I took some deep breaths and calmed myself down. I didn't want to start this tournament on the wrong foot. In fact, the tournament didn't turn out too badly at all. I started out really well and breezed through the first four rounds, as the Ganges murmuring gently in the spring. The fifth and the sixth I drew. I won the seventh game as easily as I lost the eighth and ninth. My rise and fall continued, but it was an exhilarating experience. I enjoyed each moment of testing my skills, matching my wits against my opponents'.

Meanwhile, five days had passed and two things had not yet happened. Firstly, my luggage hadn't arrived and the airlines couldn't trace it. Secondly, and worse still, Master did not call. I didn't even know the name of his village, much less his phone number there. I wouldn't be surprised if there was no phone at his home there, maybe there wasn't one in the entire village. God only knows where his village was. I had managed to pull through the first nine games and reached the quarter-finals.

Then the worst happened. On the sixth day, I was paired against Kulikov.

I called Master's home. Of course, he wasn't there to pick up the phone. I sent my dad to his place to see if he might have returned, and to find out from his neighbours if they knew about his whereabouts. But no one knew anything. I even asked dad to check with Dr D'Souza at the hospital. I remembered how the chief neurosurgeon had stood up and greeted Master with great familiarity. Dad told me that Dr D'Souza had appeared somewhat tight-lipped. In summary, no one could tell us where the hell my mentor was. And here, Kulikov was dancing on my head like a messenger of death.

Quarter-finals was a knockout round and one of us would be kicked out. I spent the whole night alternating between hope and despair. I hoped that I might win, that Master might call. I was anxious; Kulikov could wipe me clean within a few moves. To my shame, more than anything else, I dreaded the disgrace of being thrown off the chessboard so soon. I couldn't sleep the whole night. I showed up on time, red-eyed, for my match. Until stepping out of my room, I had waited for Master's call. I was going to be butchered, and for once I had hoped he'd save me in time.

Kulikov and I shook hands at the beginning of the game. He made no attempt to grip my hand or look me in the eye. He shook hands as if he couldn't care less.

'Vasu Bhatt,' I introduced myself.

He pointed at his nameplate on our table.

He was much colder than what I had read about him, and far more unfriendly than I had anticipated. Kulikov didn't wait for the game to develop but went on the offensive from the first move. Strangely, though, in the style of a beginner, he put his queen on the offence in the seventh move. I calculated and deliberated for a good twenty minutes about his thoughtless move.

What was his queen doing so early in the attack? What was Kulikov trying to do? Twenty minutes later, I made a very cautious move and the next instant, he retracted his queen, moving it back to the original position. Why did he act so dumb? It wasn't until I made my next move and went to push the button on the chess clock that I realized what he had accomplished. It was truly brilliant. He had gained a twenty-minute advantage over me.

I had wasted twenty minutes thinking over a move that had no significance. I felt stupid. It was a familiar feeling, the same one I had felt countless times while playing against Master.

Soon enough, Kulikov started with the real attack, which made me think harder and harder. I was now running around in circles thinking and rethinking my strategies before making a move. Every thought cost me a few ticks on the clock. I was feeling damp near my armpits. In the end, I was running out of time and rushing my moves.

When I realized that the game was certainly over, I looked him in the eyes, and he merely blinked to confirm. He didn't even announce the checkmate. Not that it was required, or I hadn't seen it coming, but it was the courteous thing to do.

I thought I ought to look past his rudeness to appreciate the man's genius. Just as Kulikov prepared to leave without ceremony, I mumbled without thinking: 'Any words of advice for me?'

'Take up knitting instead.'

That condescending piece of advice, even though it hurt me, didn't bother me as much as his smirk did when he uttered those words. There was that derisive tic on his lips. It was momentary, but I had noticed it.

Andrei Kulikov, knitting it is. One day, I'll watch you struggle helplessly to break free from my net. I'll weave it specially for you. Like a tiny insect you will flutter and squirm in my web before resigning yourself to your sorry fate.

Back in the hotel room when I analysed my moves, I saw that my own game had not been bad at all. I had a real chance against Kulikov had I a bit more time to calculate the last few moves. Had I not lost twenty minutes on that one move, I could have given him a tough fight. I might even have drawn. Or at least it *felt* that way.

Seeing how close I was, thinking about where I could have been, I felt increasingly angry. I was out of the tournament at the first knockout stage. But I was more sorry than angry. Sorry because I was knocked out. It could have been avoided. Every time the round ended, I returned to my corner only to find there was no one to pull my mouth guard out, give me a sip of water, wipe my sweat, or to whisper something, anything, in my ear. Anything. Anything at all. He should have been there. My master. He just wasn't there.

What was the pressing urgency for Master to leave for his village? Who had died anyway? He could have at least called home to find out how was I doing in the tournaments. But, no, why would the Great Master dismount his high horse for a loser like me? What kind of a master was he, who always left me to fend for myself in major tournaments?

I stayed back in my room on the seventh day rather than watch Kulikov turn his opponents to pulp. I didn't feel like going to the venue in the same set of clothes. I had nearly made up my mind to buy new clothes. But thanks to the helpful Punjabi-speaking officer, my luggage was traced after all. It had been at the airport all this while. What my tiny suitcase was doing in the oversized baggage section was something no one could explain. At any rate, I was relieved to get it back.

I ordered room service because at least the hotel staff spoke English. Feeling bored, and to distract myself from the constant onslaught of angry thoughts about my absentee master, I turned on the television. But there wasn't much to watch as it was all in Spanish. Nevertheless, I paused at a music channel. Skinny girls were bouncing around in skimpy clothes. It was a decent distraction – until the face of Master flashed in front of me again. He just hadn't bothered to call. Not at all.

Just then, the phone rang.

I swear, he's had it now.

'Hello?' I said, irritated.

'Did you miss me?'

'Oh, Rea? So, uh I was just rushing out. I—'

I was in no mood for sympathy, even if it came from Rea.

'You never called.'

'I'd called you the day I landed! It's just been very hectic.'

Sensing my anger, she spoke pensively, 'You lost, didn't you?'

'You think I'm just a loser who can never win, don't you?'

'I was just—'

There was a knock on the door. My pizza had arrived.

'Someone's at the door, Rea. Hold.'

A waiter walked in and placed the tray on the table.

'Enjoy your pizza,' he said while walking out.

'Yes, Rea,' I resumed.

'Didn't you say you were rushing out?'

'Uh … I was.'

'But I heard someone say, "enjoy your pizza".'

This was followed by an awkward pause.

'You didn't have to lie to me, Vasu,' she said. 'I waited for your call every day.'

'Did I ask you to wait?'

I'd never envisaged shouting at Rea, but I don't know what got into me. 'Did I promise to call you every day? And even if I did, it's not like people don't break their promises. Ask my master if you like.'

'Why are you shouting at me?'

'I'm *not* shouting,' I screamed. 'Just leave me alone, will you?'

'Vasu…' Rea was crying. And she put the phone down.

I hit the receiver on my forehead. Twice, thrice, and again. It hurt. I felt my skin stretch. I touched it and it was a bit bumpy. I spent the next twenty minutes calling her back. She didn't come to the phone. Her father answered every time and I would just disconnect. I would have kept calling all night, but each one was an international call and even a 'hello' was more than the price of a coke and chips.

I stayed in my room the whole of the next day, waiting for Rea's call. Tried calling her again a few times, but only her dad picked up the phone. Mother called the next day to ask how I was doing, if I was getting proper food in a foreign country, yada-yada-yada. I made her put the phone down. Varun called, Mira called. I treated everyone equally – rudely.

But Master didn't call.

The flight back home was the worst, for I sat preparing myself for the damage I had done. The money that was lost, the love that I had pushed aside and the missing master who couldn't care less.

'Vasu!' mother exclaimed as soon as I entered home. 'Your dad just stepped out to get hot gulab jamuns for you. He said you would like it with the kheer.'

'I'm not hungry, mother.' I left my suitcase near the door.

'How did it go, Vasu?' she asked cautiously.

'I'm tired, mum.'

'Have something to eat first! I've made pulao, raita, shahi-paneer, urad dal and, of course, kheer on slow simmer.'

'Did he call? Master?'

'He only returned last night. Your father met him,' she said, offering me lemon-and-mint water. 'Have your dinner first and I'll tell you.'

'No, I don't want to know or eat anything. I'm sleepy, mum,' I said heading towards my room. I slammed the door shut behind me.

Muffin was moving about in her bowl as always. My side table was clean since Bajrang Bali was still in my suitcase. Varun's bed was vacant, as it had been for long. My bed was neatly done. Clean pillows and a new bed sheet. I threw my rucksack on the floor and hurled my shoes at the wall. Socks as well. Jacket, shirt and jeans too. Snuggling up in my bed, I tried to sleep.

I couldn't.

I had hoped to come back a champion from Linares. There would have been a grand celebration tonight. I would have bought gifts for mother and Rea with the prize money. How proud my parents and my master would have been! But none of that happened because I had lost. How I hated myself, how mad I was at myself – more than I had ever been at Master. I felt like a sealed can of cola that had been shaken vigorously. Waiting and wanting to explode.

The door opened. Dad came and sat beside me. I pretended to be asleep. Stroking my hair, he softly whispered my name. I didn't open my eyes. He kissed my forehead and went around the room, collecting my stuff that lay littering. From the corner of my eye, I saw him quietly carrying my clothes and shoes out of the room. Then he gently closed the door.

I burst into tears.

I wanted to tell everyone I had hurt that even though it might seem that way, I wasn't being mean deliberately. I had tried to be brave at Linares. I had come to terms with the fact that I was on my own there. But I don't think it was too much to ask that Master be available to at least speak to.

I cried till I could cry no more. I thought I would fall asleep crying, but exactly the reverse happened. It left me wide awake. I was really hungry. So much so that my stomach began hurting from hunger. Master's, Rea's, everyone's face flashed in front of me, followed by all the items mother had cooked. Pulao, kheer, paneer, raita, dal, gulab jamun, pudina paratha. I glanced up at the clock. Five hours had passed. The parents must be fast asleep.

I opened the door quietly and entered the kitchen. Mother would always do the dishes at night before going to sleep. She said she couldn't bear to wake up to a dirty kitchen. But tonight there were no clean dishes next to the sink. There were no dirty ones either. I opened the fridge. The curries in the bowls were full. The pack of gulab jamuns lay sealed. Everything was untouched. My hunger disappeared instantly when I realized that my parents hadn't eaten either.

'Vasu?' mother said softly from behind. 'It's cold and you are in your boxers!'

'You haven't eaten, mother? Neither of you have.'

'Go, put on something warm first,' she said.

'Why didn't you wake me up?'

'I'll go get your woollens.'

'Mother!' I held her wrist. 'I'm sorry. I really am. I didn't—'

'First you wear your jumper, eat something, and then we'll talk.' She was adamant, and for once, I did what I was told.

'Mum, say *something*...'

'Your father was very sad, Vasu,' she murmured. 'He said he couldn't bear to see you so down.'

'Is he asleep?'

She just nodded.

'Let's all eat together,' I said. 'I'll wake him up.'

'It's midnight, Vasu.'

'You just heat up the dinner.'

Suddenly a smile broke out on her beautiful, gentle face.

'I'll make fresh dough!'

I went into their room. Dad was sleeping peacefully. I don't think he was pretending like I had when he'd come to me. His spectacles were resting on a book on the side table. Next to it was a copper glass full of water. It was one of those Ayurvedic habits he followed without fail: fill a glass of copper with water at night and have it first thing in the morning. I gently stroked his hair like he had stroked mine. It had gone thin over the years, I realized. I kissed him on his cheek. He woke up.

'Papa?' I said.

'Vasu?' He got up immediately and reached out for his specs. He looked to his left to see if mother was still sleeping, and then saw the light outside.

'Your mother's in the kitchen?'

'Let's have dinner, papa.'

'Are you okay, Vasu?'

'I am now.'

'Don't let chess affect you like this, Vasu,' he said while turning on the table lamp. 'Don't ever let anything affect you like this.' Then he started speaking as if he had not been sleeping a few seconds ago. 'Winning and losing are twins joined at the hip, son. They are two sides of the same coin. One tournament is not the end of the world. There's always a next time. Ultimately, what matters is not whether you won or lost, but if you tried your best. Don't be too hard on yourself.'

As he sat there in his vest, I felt strangely protective and concerned about him. I sensed his vulnerability and my own power to hurt him.

'Okay, but first let's have dinner, dad.'

'Promise me first that you won't take defeats to your heart. Play it like a game, Vasu.'

'I promise, I'll really try,' I said. 'Let's eat something now.'

As always, he went into the kitchen to help mother and set up the table.

'You sit,' I said. 'I'll set up everything.'

We spent the next two hours at the dinner table. I recounted my experiences at Linares. Every bite of food, every word uttered by dad, every smile on mother's face, repaired me a bit. Deep within, though, none of it made me feel any less guilty. I wished they weren't so nice to me. At least, I would have some solace or justification for behaving the way I had. But here they were, so welcoming. Meeting their truant son with open arms. Even though I bit them like a rattled snake, they still picked me up and caressed me. Maybe all parents are like that, accepting their stubborn children back, or maybe not. At any rate, I was deeply ashamed of myself.

None of this meant that Master was right to abandon me like that. I had a score to settle. But I had to apologize to Varun and Mira first. I couldn't wait for dawn so I could call them. Most of all, though, I had to call Rea. I had to see her and make up with her before meeting Master. Of course, I was desperate to see Master, but I also wanted to make it quite clear that I was in no hurry to see him either. I didn't want to go rushing to him first thing in the morning. I did want to, but I didn't.

I called Mira first and her soothing voice and encouraging words immediately put me at ease. 'Master must have a reason, Vasu,' she said. 'Let's not read between the lines or make quick judgements. Maybe he's preparing you so that you're independent.' She went on to tell me that losing this tournament was not the end of the world and that I ought to take it a bit easy. 'The hand that's always clutched gets tired very quickly,' she added wisely. I felt the guilt of losing subside but as always it was Varun who would crack me up. I called him. He spoke as if nothing had happened.

'I'm sorry, bro,' I said. 'I didn't speak to you properly that day.'

'Munshiji,' he said gravely, 'don't get formal with me. Besides, who doesn't know that even a goldfish communicates better than a chess player?' And he started laughing.

'I *am* a good communicator!'

'Oh yeah? Is that why Rea isn't exactly boiling over with love for you right now?'

'Rea?' I jumped out of my seat. 'How do you know?'

'Let's say, she trusts yours truly more than she trusts you.'

'How should I pacify her ... how can I win her back, Varun?'

'Love is not a game of chess, Vasu, that you can just lose or win based on the last move. She cried her eyes out the day she called me. Don't hurt her. You can do better.'

You can do better. These words kept ringing in my ears. I must do better. I had no excuse to not do better. But what about Master? Couldn't he do better too?

I didn't lose in Linares because everyone else was better than me. I had lost because my lighthouse went out on me when I needed it most. He wasn't there to steer my ship through the storm; he had just left me to crash against the waves and break little by little. I was lost at sea and he hadn't even come looking for me, not even once in the four years that I had known him. I cast Master out of my mind for the time being. It hurt to think about it.

I met Rea for lunch. Other than a 'hi', I didn't say anything for quite some time. I didn't know how to face her. What would I say to her?

'Are you going to give me those flowers,' she said, 'or take them back home with you?'

Like Varun, she was behaving as if nothing had happened. Without saying a word, I handed her the bouquet of red roses. And the two chocolate bars I'd brought for her from Linares.

'Wow!' she exclaimed. 'You got me chocolates from Spain!'

'I'm sorry for the other day, Rea. I was such a jerk. I wish I wasn't in your life. I—'

'Sh!' She put her finger on my lips. 'Never say that again, Vasu.'

I peered into her hazel eyes. They had suddenly become more serious, a bit smaller.

'You don't know what it's like to not have your loved ones around, Vasu. You are all that I have. I can't talk to my brother. And there isn't much that I can share with my parents.'

She got up from her seat and hugged me tight, her smooth face against my stubble. I was over the moon. I loosened up as she laughed and spoke of innocuous things.

I wasn't as good as Varun, but I did a small mimicry of Kulikov, especially the way he would not smile and refuse to shake hands. Rea was in splits.

We had chana bhaturas for lunch and I went straight to Master's after that. He opened the door at the first bell. As usual, he was calm, unfrazzled.

'How are you, Vasu? Let's look at your games.'

'You didn't ask if I won or not?'

'You aren't exactly walking in with a trophy.'

'And why do you think that is?'

'Because you lost more games than you won,' he said coldly. 'Cola?'

'No, that's not why,' I said a bit loudly. 'I lost because you were not there.'

'Oh please, not again!' He rolled his eyes.

Master had a way of setting me off. All this while I still hadn't learned to accept his indifference towards me, my fate and my life. No matter how much I reminded myself that he didn't owe me anything, or that I was the student here, or that he was an old man, nothing would work. He could hurt me with hardly a word at all. Real bad.

'It's the truth, all right?' I could feel myself foaming at the mouth. 'I lost because you were not there.'

'I told you that I would not join you for any tournament. Besides, I don't like talking on the phone. It gives me a headache.'

'Bullshit!' I let loose. 'You didn't call because you didn't *want* to call. You never go to any tournament with me because you just don't give a shit about me or anyone else for that matter.'

'That's not true,' he replied.

'Of course it's true! That's why you are living here alone, old man. No one calls you, no one visits you, and you have no friends. That's why—'

'Vasu, that's enough!'

'—that's why you have no son, no daughter, no wife, no family.'

'Vasu!' he roared.

He got up from his seat. His lips were quivering. There was fire in his eyes. But it died down pretty quickly. He sat back in his chair, calm again.

'I thought you *were* my family,' he mumbled after a silence of a good few minutes. He took off his glasses and rested his head in his hands.

'I'm not lonely by choice, you know,' he spoke after many minutes.

I had calmed down somewhat by now.

'I'm a terrible student, Master,' I said. Holding him by his wrists, I sat down next to him. His eyes looked old and moist. 'You know I was angry and I didn't mean to say those things.'

'No, Vasu,' he said. 'I shouldn't leave you wondering any more. It's time you hear why I don't accompany you to any tournament.'

'I don't know why I've turned so bitter, Master. I'm hurting everyone.'

I was having such a hard time dealing with my own reality that I wasn't sure if I could handle the one from Master's life as well.

'Vasu,' he gestured for me to sit. 'You should know my story.'

I faintly recollected reading somewhere, 'don't poke the wild one'. It was a little too late for that now. The sleeping lion was stretching already. Majestically.

12

THE LOST QUEEN

I WAS BORN in 1911. My mother was always after me with a stick because I was a naughty child breaking earthen pots, ruining her pickles drying in the sun, causing a dust storm in the neighbour's yard spoiling their freshly washed laundry or roughing up their children. Someone was always knocking on our door with a complaint or two.

Unlike mother, though, father was a gentleman. Only once did he get mad at me. It was the harvesting season and I sneaked into our neighbour's pen and let their cattle loose. The livestock ruined their wheat fields. This act was almost sacrilegious, for crops are dearer to a farmer than his own life. Father gave me a sound beating and he stopped only when mother intervened. He was the only son of his parents and my grandfather had been the only son of his. A sole heir, an only son – it had been going on like this for more than five generations.

Mother couldn't conceive even after six years of their marriage. My father was under immense pressure to bring home another wife so that a son could continue the lineage and look after our fields. But he wouldn't agree. He loved my mother deeply.

One late evening, a sadhu came for alms. Smeared in ash, he was carrying a trident. Being an ardent devotee of Shiva himself, father honoured him and requested him to stay overnight. Strangely, the sadhu was fond of playing chess and carried a set in his bag. He invited my father to a game. A giant glass of sweetened milk, full of cashews, almonds and sultanas and, seasoned with saffron was placed next to him, which he would sip after each move. My mother fanned him reverently while they played chess. Father gave him a tough fight but lost eventually.

'Shiva Shiva Shankara. Shiva Shiva Shankara,' he bellowed in joy, and said, 'I'm very happy. Ask for a boon.'

My parents fell at his feet but said nothing.

'You want a son,' he said firmly, 'don't you?'

Out of reverence, my parents spoke nothing and remained prostrated.

'So be it,' he said, and gave a pinch of holy ash to my mother. 'Drink milk from this glass for the next forty days,' he added, and handed his glass to my mother.

Ten months later, I was born.

'A healthy baby, thankfully, with no horns,' my father would often joke as he'd tell me the story of my birth.

The celebrations had gone on for days. My grandparents, parents, sixty cows, eight pairs of bulls, five dogs, two parrots, three cats and a mongoose, we all lived in a big house surrounded by acres and acres of our land. At a distance of about thirty metres were the staff quarters where fourteen families lived tending to our fields and cattle.

Mother could not conceive any more children after me. Many villagers suggested that my father remarry so I could have a sibling. The child mortality rate was high during those times and nearly half the children would never make it beyond twelve or thirteen years of age. Just like my grandfather, though, my father never brought another woman home.

'I would never do that to you,' he would say to my mother.

I was pampered by everyone, especially my father and our workers. Life was most amazing sitting under the peepul tree and eating delicious mangoes, peeling succulent sugarcane, swimming in the river and eating roasted corn. Sometimes I would just sit on one of the cows while it bathed in the river. But, above all, my favourite activity was to watch my father play chess and win. Even the village chief, who was an accomplished player too, rarely ever won a game against him.

I would not let my father play until he agreed that he would play with me after finishing his game. Sometimes I would just fall asleep in his lap while his games dragged on. It was the most beautiful thing, Vasu. Especially in winters when they would play around a bonfire. How I loved the delirious smell of the freshly roasted peanuts, the crackling fire, and starry skies. I would cover myself with a blanket.

I was eight years old and had just started going to the village school. Although I was old enough, my grandparents didn't want me to go to school. In those days, parents preferred to look after their kids at home. The men would work in the fields while the women would tend to the cattle. It was a simple life.

Every morning, mother would give me a glassful of hot milk mixed with jaggery, two big chapattis drenched in butter, and pickle. I loved jaggery. I always asked for some more on the side.

'If I keep feeding you like this, it will become impossible to catch you,' she would say lovingly. 'You already climb up the tree after your pranks.'

'Why, don't you want your son to be strong?' I would joke.

'With all the trouble you cause, Nandu, I think you are strong enough.'

I walked to school which was four kilometres away. I would take a big piece of jaggery to lick and chew on the way. Two of my favourite dogs, Kalu and Goblu, would follow me and see me off all the way to the school. When out of my mother's sight, I would often let them lick the jaggery, especially towards the end. They loved licking it off my palms. Those selfish buggers never came to pick me up, though.

Father would secretly give me money so I could buy sweetmeats during lunch. The same hawker would wait for me outside our school. On a bicycle, he would be carrying a wooden box with small compartments showcasing different sweetmeats. Mother strongly disapproved of wasting money like that, but father made sure I could buy sweetmeats every day.

One day, it was drizzling outside. My mother fed me as usual, and asked me not to go to school since the weather was a little muggy. As usual, I paid no attention to her and insisted on going to school. I was in no mood to skip my candyfloss. The principal and the two teachers never bothered much with teaching. I even recall them playing cards and smoking beedis in the shade of the tree. All day, we would study for an hour at the most. Almost everyone's parents were illiterate; so they had no way of knowing what was going on. And we thought even an hour was too much.

Education didn't have a major role in our lives anyway. We certainly didn't need it to rear our cattle, to cook food, or to know what seeds to sow in which season. People didn't need architects or masons; they built their own houses. The vocation of a plumber didn't exist because there were no taps. We had wells. There was no electricity in our village. There was just one physician and he had never been to any school, ever. Yet, he would give herbal concoctions and extracts that could infuse life even in the dead, so to speak. There were no veterinary doctors, as our cattle rarely fell ill, and even when they did, the same physician who treated us would treat our cattle. There were no pesticides, weedicides or artificial fertilizers. All in all, school wasn't the most important place for learning – it was for playing, though.

That day started no differently. Kalu and Goblu saw me off to the school as usual. We were playing in the school courtyard. The cool breeze of the morning had turned into a violent windstorm. So, rather than studying under the tree – something that we did on most mornings and sunny winter days – our teachers called us into the room.

Bhiku, one of the workers in the village, came to get me. I couldn't say what time it was because we didn't have any clocks in the school. Only the teachers had wrist watches. He whispered to my class teacher, who called out my name. I stood up. 'Pack your bag and go home,' he said. I didn't think much of it. Bhiku rushed to close my inkpot, and kept my slate and pen in my bag. Lifting me in his arms, he dashed to his bicycle. He sat me on the front bar and pedalled fast and hard.

'What happened?' I asked.

He wouldn't say a word.

'Speak up, Bhiku,' I said. 'What happened?'

'Nothing. They just want you at home.'

As soon as we neared the edge of our land, he haphazardly left his bike under the tree, lifted me in his arms again and ran to the house. As we went through the fields, I could see my home at a distance. It looked as if a number of people were visiting. A few steps forward and I could hear wailing. It was common for women to come and wail loudly upon anyone's death in the village. My heart pounded.

I hope I haven't lost grandfather or grandmother; they were perfectly fine when I left for school in the morning.

I tugged hard at his shirt, 'Tell me, what happened?'

The sound of wailing was growing louder as we got closer. The whole village was there. As soon as I entered, my father took me from Bhiku's arms. I remember feeling scared and nervous. I looked around. I just wanted to make sure both my grandparents were okay. I saw my grandfather sitting with other men. Then I looked in the direction where all the women were sitting, and there she was, safe and sound, my grandmother. She was wailing too. I suddenly felt a deep hollow in the pit of my stomach.

'Where's mother?' I tilted my head back a little to look at my father who was holding me tightly in his arms while I was looking over his shoulder.

He looked at me, ran his hand through my hair and face, and hugged me tightly again.

'Where is she?' I shouted.

He didn't answer. Just then, next to where grandmother was sitting, I saw a body lying on the floor at a distance. It was my mother, covered with a white cloth till her neck.

I tried to push myself away from my father and started beating his chest with my fists. 'Let me go, let me go, put me down.'

He put me down. I ran towards her and threw my arms around her.

Her body was stiff and cold, her face blue.

When I insisted on knowing what happened, they told me that she died of a snake bite in the farm.

Even today, I still I think that had I not gone to school that day, perhaps none of this would have happened. Because whenever I was home, she would always be busy looking after me and would never get the time to do much else. Had I been home, she would have sent one of the workers to the fields instead of going there herself. She would have lived.

I'm seventy-five now and I still miss her. Badly.

My father never remarried, but he wanted me betrothed as soon as I turned fourteen. I was drawn to chess, though. So I was able to postpone the event. But finally, at twenty, I was married to a beautiful girl four years younger to me. Her name was Uma Devi. She was a stark contrast to my mother, mostly quiet and always shy. She took care of my father, my grandparents and me. I got her addicted to cola, but she would never drink it in front of my father or grandparents, but only in our room. She had soft brown eyes, and long hair that fell to her knees. Uma's small round face was as beautiful as it was smooth.

She was my lucky charm, Vasu. From the moment she stepped into our house, I progressed rapidly. Winning one tournament after the other, setting new records, scaling new heights, the chess world began to take note of me. I was mostly out playing tournaments and would be gone for long. Whether I played a tournament in another city or country, I almost always brought her a gift. She had no requirements. Whether I got her a plain sari or a silver ring, she was happy with anything. Happier still was she to see me.

Sometimes... often, in fact, sitting next to an oil lamp, I would simply play practice games late into the night. In villages, people sleep early because they have to wake up at dawn and there's no time during the day to rest. But she would remain awake for as long as I was up even though she knew nothing about chess herself. Whenever I asked her to go to sleep, she would shake her head and tell me that she didn't want to waste a moment even blinking when I was around.

(*Master's eyes held a spark as he spoke of his wife, as if he were living it right then. There was an eagerness in his speech, a glow on his face. His hands were animated. He was no longer stooping in his chair but leaning forward to ensure that I wouldn't miss a word. I couldn't recall the last time he had spoken about anyone or anything as excitedly. Not even chess.*)

But I was so engrossed in playing chess and winning tournaments that I didn't really spend any time with her. I regret it to this day, Vasu. She just stood by me like a rock, whereas I never took her to any pilgrimage, nor to the village fair. I never sat down and had a meal with her. She would serve me hot food, fresh chapattis, and I would just start pushing pawns immediately after my dinner. She had no friends or anyone of her age group in our family. There was only so much she could share with the female workers in the field. Yet, she never complained, nor did she say a word. I wish she *had* complained and demanded me for things that made her happy. I wouldn't have been so blind to life then.

She would wait patiently for me while I was overseas or out of town. Upon my return, she would always wait till I was well rested and well fed before telling me all that happened in the village in my absence. I would busy myself analysing my games from the tournament while she would keep on chatting. She knew that I was barely listening, but it didn't matter to her.

I got my GM title when I was twenty-three. As—

(*'Wow! You are a GM!' I couldn't control my surprise. But he continued in his matter-of-fact tone.*)

As it had been with my mother, Uma too wasn't able to conceive even after six years of our marriage. I got the same suggestions from others that my father had got – marry another woman. I once joked with Uma, asking her what if I brought a second wife.

'What second? Third,' she said. '*I'm* the second wife.'

I looked at her, intrigued.

'Chess is your first wife,' she added.

And we both laughed.

'But will you, really?' she asked me in a sombre tone, lowering her head.

'Never, Uma,' I said. 'You are the first and last woman in my life.'

A few more years passed and I turned twenty-seven. One day, I returned from an international tournament that I had lost miserably. I was quite distressed, more than you are at losing in Linares, Vasu. Uma had that look in her eyes, something I can't explain. Some day, you will know what I mean.

'No chess tonight,' she said after I had napped in the afternoon and had my dinner.

'I must annotate my tournament games, Uma. I lost badly,' I said, and opened up the chessboard.

'You will be a father soon,' she gently broke the news to me.

I forgot all about chess, Vasu. I hadn't felt as happy even when I got the GM title. I lifted her in my arms and danced in joy.

'Careful, careful,' she said.

I put her down on the bed.

'Promise me one thing,' she said. 'Be it a boy or a girl, you'll make our child a world chess champion.'

'You, Uma' I exclaimed. '*You* are saying this?'

I would like our child to be a genius like you.

During her pregnancy, in the third month, my grandfather passed away. Grandmother felt that the child in the womb had brought bad luck, and so she consulted some astrologers and tantriks. One of the astrologers told her to immerse the horns of a goat in the Ganges. This would set things right, he said. The child would be very lucky for the mother but portentous for me, the father. Only the horns of a goat could save us, he reiterated.

'I don't want this child,' Uma said to me after hearing of the prophecy. 'Anyone who harms you has no place in my life.'

It took a great deal of talking to placate her. I reminded her that the astrologer had said that if we did as he said, all would be well. Granny went ahead with the remedy as prescribed by the astrologer but, in a bizarre accident, slipped and, before anyone could do anything, she was swept away by the strong current. The horns of a goat couldn't save her.

Uma became even more paranoid. She would not let me step out. I told her that God was greater than any astrologer, but she wouldn't stop worrying. The environment at home became tense and sad. Nevertheless, we were desperately waiting for the child now, especially my father and I. Both of us wanted a girl, but Uma wanted a boy. It had been very long since we had had any good news at all. The world championship was fast approaching too.

I had already missed a couple of major tournaments because Uma wouldn't let me leave the village. But there was no way I was going to miss playing the world championships. It was after decades of hard work that I had qualified to play for the ultimate title. FIDE, the current governing chess body, had little influence at the time. My opponent was directly decided upon recommendation by chess veterans based on our rankings. It was going to be with Alekhine.

(*'Alekhine?' I shouted. 'The Alexander Alekhine?'*

Master nodded.

'You've seen him in flesh and blood?'

'I beat him, Vasu.'

'Master!' I jumped up.

'But it wasn't worth it,' he said in his solemn voice. Unmoved, he continued as if it wasn't Alekhine but a student he'd defeated.)

Some more months passed and I was all set to leave.

'Trust my sixth sense,' Uma said to me. 'Please don't go. There's no one around. The baby will be born any day.'

'Uma,' I said, 'you are worrying about nothing. It's only the beginning of the seventh month and I'll be back in the eighth. Your delivery is almost three months away.'

'I don't want you to travel,' she said. 'The astrologer had said the child is not good for you.'

'I've to play Alekhine, Uma,' I insisted. 'The whole world will laugh at me if I abandon the match.'

She began crying, but I had no intention of forgoing the championship. I consoled her somehow and left for Mumbai two days later. My ship was to leave for Leningrad from the Mumbai port.

Between my practice sessions on the ship, I kept thinking about Uma and our soon-to-arrive child. I was feeling guilty about leaving her when she needed me the most. She had always been there for me. She had loved me with her heart and soul, but when it was my turn, I chose chess over her. I thought I would buy her a nice gift, a Russian fur coat. What a scene it would be if I took her to the village fair in a fur coat. No one would have even seen anything like that in the village. She would surely be shy to put it on, but I knew I'd be able to talk her into wearing it.

But, Vasu, always remember, the more intimate a relationship, the less it is about things or gifts. It's always the small gestures that make all the difference. Some action that shows you understand, care and love. Words that make the other person feel wanted, important and loved. And gifts often fail at conveying that message.

Though she didn't know anything about chess, she would insist that I tell her stories of my tournaments. She would sit in rapt attention and whenever I narrated a story of my victory, she would go, 'Of course, who can beat you; you are the best.' But whenever I told her how I lost, she would say, 'You must have been tired, or are you sure the opponent didn't play any tricks or cast a spell on you?' She would take some salt and red chillies and draw imaginary circles with it before I left home in order to ward off any evil forces.

Uma's love completed me. Chess was more beautiful because of my wife's presence in my life. I wanted to win the championship not only for myself but also for her, for my father, and our future child. I wanted Uma to feel that she had indeed married a legend. I wanted my father to know that his son was an icon. I wanted the village to see the emperor among them, that I was the best out there. There's nothing beyond winning a world championship for a chess player – this was the belief I strongly held at the time.

Twenty-six games later, Alekhine and I were playing for the winning point in the final game. He had the advantage of playing white. I opted for Phildor's defence but, somewhere in the middle, his D-pawn began to really bother me. There was no doubt that his position was stronger. There was no strategic loophole when it came to someone like Alekhine, but there was a tactical advantage I had exploited all along. It was something I knew about Alekhine. Something that was both his strength and weakness – he was an aggressive and impatient player.

I went for a closed game, avoiding exchange of pieces and locking the centre. Our knights and bishops were in the play but mostly blocked. Even forty moves later, only two pawns had been exchanged. Our rooks were closely guarding our kings, and our queens were struggling to make any play on that clogged board. I kept my cool while Alekhine became increasingly frustrated even if he wouldn't show it. But he sacrificed his knight for two pawns, only so he could open up the board. That one move cost him the game, and the title.

Overnight, I became an international sensation in chess circles and they featured me on Russian TV. I sent a telegram home announcing that I had won, along with details of my arrival. At the Mumbai port, Uma's brother came to receive me. I wasn't expecting national media or too many reporters, but I didn't think that not one journalist would show up to report on my victory.

I hugged Ramesh with a wide grin but he showed no signs of joy.

'What's the matter?' I asked him.

'We've to go to the hospital.'

'Why, what happened?'

'She's a little unwell.'

'Who? Uma?'

Other than a brief nod, Ramesh didn't give out too many details. When I insisted on knowing more, he said everything was under control. The hospital was six hours away from my village. But the village itself was a two-day train journey from where we were currently. We hired a taxi instead to get there faster. Still, it would take us almost thirty hours.

Just before reaching the hospital, Ramesh told me that Uma had had a premature delivery. She gave birth to a baby boy.

'A boy!' I screamed in unrestrained happiness. 'Why didn't you tell me earlier?'

'But … he was stillborn.'

'What?'

'And Uma has internal bleeding.'

I held him by the arms and shook him hard.

'What are you saying, Ramesh?'

'She doesn't know yet that the child is no more,' he said. 'She thinks he's in incubation.'

'Please say it's not true, Ramesh.'

He just kept quiet, but I broke down.

Everyone from her family was at the hospital. My father too. They were all silent and downcast.

'Where's Uma?'

They pointed towards the ICU and I ran. When I barged in, a nurse came running behind me, asking me to get out of the ICU, but there was no way I would do that. She called the doctor so I could be talked out of sitting inside the ICU.

'What happened to my wife?' I cried, clasping the doctor's hands. 'Will she be all right?'

The doctor took me outside.

'It was a difficult and painful delivery,' he said. 'There's massive internal bleeding.'

'Will she be all right?'

'It's in God's hands,' he replied. 'She regains her consciousness briefly, mutters your name, asks about the baby and loses consciousness again.'

I went inside the ICU. Dragging my chair closer to Uma, I stroked her beautiful face and waited for her to open her eyes. I held her hand in mine and kept looking at her. She looked peaceful but tired. It was the first time that she wasn't wearing any lipstick. There was no bindi on her forehead, no sindoor in the parting of her hair. There was no mangalsutra around her neck. I had never seen her without all those symbols of marriage, but that day she looked very different. Like a little girl.

'Oh God, if you make her okay, I'll never play chess again,' I prayed.

'How could I leave her behind for chess? Why didn't I listen to her?' I thought.

'Did you win?' A feeble voice broke into my thoughts.

'Uma?' I shouted with joy. 'Are you okay?'

'Did you win?' she said, smiling faintly. 'How's our son?'

'Please forgive—'

'Sshh…' she mumbled. 'You don't need to be sorry.'

'I'll never leave you alone like that again.'

'Did you wi—'

'Yes, Uma, I won, I won.'

'Our son?'

'He's also okay.'

'I don't think I'll live. I can feel my life fleeing out of me. I see death, I—'

'No, Uma, no.' I couldn't control my tears. 'You'll be just fine. I know it. You've to play with our son, don't you?'

'Promise me,' she said, 'you'll make him a world champion like you.'

'Yes, Uma, I promise. Please be okay.'

'What if you leave me again for the first woman?' She smiled. She was softly gasping in between.

'I promise, Uma, I'll never play a tournament again. I'll never even go and watch one.'

'Liar!' She chuckled. 'How will he become a champion if you never accompany him on a tournament?'

She gasped.

'I want to be with you, with our son,' she said. 'I don't want to die.'

I pressed her hand firmly.

'Nothing's wrong with you, Uma.'

'I think I'm going...' she barely managed to utter. 'I don't want to.' A tear trickled down her eye.

She was struggling to breathe, gasping more and more. Then she began convulsing. I ran out to get the doctor.

'Help!' I screamed in the corridor. 'Help! My wife's dying.'

A team of doctors rushed in and they asked me to stay out. Nurses ran in and out of the ICU. They tried but all attempts at reviving her failed.

(*Master sat there, quiet. Utterly quiet. I hadn't the courage to speak either.*)

'My own queen checkmated me, Vasu,' he said, chuckling.

'And that's the difference between real life and chess,' he added. 'Unlike chess, it's not your opponent but your loved ones who conquer you, corner you and checkmate you. My whole life with Uma felt like a game. One I had lost.'

(*Master got up, pushed the table aside and paced up and down the room. He looked heavenwards and took a deep breath.*)

'Do you know what Uma used to say? If we have a daughter, we'll name her Vaishnavi,' Master said without waiting for my answer. 'And if it's a boy, we'll name him ... Vasu.'

13

PAWNED

'THE FIRST TIME I saw you at the tournament,' Master said, 'I noticed how eagerly you were watching the board. I saw how you were trying to read me, provoke me. I saw your impatient eyes. And when I read your name on the pairing sheet … Vasu … I knew. Here was my chance to make good on the promise I had made to Uma.'

'What if I fail you, Master?'

'Not in this lifetime,' Master said without blinking.

'Two questions have been nagging me, Master,' I said.

'Don't you think you broke your promise to her by coming to my tournament all those years ago?'

'It was Uma's birthday. I had to go. I had to find a Vasu. And look what a birthday gift you turned out to be!' A faint smile played on his lips momentarily.

I lowered my head. Had Master not shared his past, I would have never known that there was an ocean of love and emotions inside him.

'And how come Anand Sharma is not listed as a world champion?'

'Nandan Nath Upadhyaya is.' Master paused and then added, 'I'm Nandan Nath Upadhyaya, Vasu. I changed my name to Anand Sharma after Uma passed away, and moved far away from my village to this small town to lead a quiet and obscure life.'

Of course. It all made sense now. Till date, the chess world occasionally brought up the topic of the mysterious disappearance of the world chess champion of 1938. The chess prodigy Nandan Upadhyaya who was a world champion at twenty-seven.

'My disappearance had been a heated topic, but with the beginning of the World War II a few months later, it died a quick death,' Master said. 'Besides, in a country struggling for independence, the absence or presence of a chess champion wasn't even noticed, much less reported.'

'That's not true, Master, many of your wins and strategies are quoted till date. Oh Master, I'm so foolish. I should never have questioned you.'

'I'm too old, Vasu,' Master said, taking a deep breath. 'I don't know how long I'll be around, but let me give you a golden rule of thumb. Whenever you are stuck in any tournament, simply ask yourself, "What would Master do?" and you'll know what step to take. I promise.'

Today, Master looked more peaceful than I had seen him in a long time. It was as if a big weight had been lifted off him. I rode all the way back home with his story running in my head. The son that Master never had a chance to hold in his arms, he saw in me. For the last five years, he had taught me without charging a single penny. And what had I given him in return?

Every time I had lost, like a petulant child, I found a way to blame it on him. I had been living in my selfish little cocoon, having father, mother, Master, Rea, everyone at my beck and call. The great Vasu would holler and everyone would just come running, because, come on, Vasu was going to be a GM someday and everyone must do as he wishes!

I vowed that moment to reinvent myself, to man up and to wholeheartedly devote everything I had to every game I would ever play. I owed it to all those who had loved and put up with me all these years. I had a debt to pay. And there was not a moment to lose.

Over the next two years, while I didn't win every tournament, I won a lot more than I ever had before. Not only did it make Master happy, but my victories also gave a tremendous boost to my self-confidence. I no longer got the shivers when playing against a GM or any other player. Hell, I went on to earn the coveted GM title myself at the age of twenty-one.

Of course, I didn't earn that title overnight. It wasn't like I won one game and suddenly I was GM. It was a result of all the wins I consistently registered, which in turn earned me a certain rating, qualifying me for the title. It was a slow, painstaking process of watching your rating go up and down, stagnate and then climb again. I was thrilled to be a GM, but for some time now all I wanted was the real thing – the world chess champion title.

But the day FIDE informed me that I had qualified for the GM title, Varun and Mira insisted that it was time for a celebration. All of the hungama at home, and my parents' happy faces thrilled me, of course, but I also saw clearly what my true aim was. My real redemption lay in defeating Andrei Kulikov. If reports were to be believed, Kulikov, the reigning world champion, had become even more elusive and conceited. He was now rarely seen at international tournaments.

Kulikov had said in no uncertain terms that he would only appear to compete for world championships. This was quite unusual – all world champions before him had continued to play other tournaments too. But not Andrei Kulikov. He was cut from a different cloth. It was a matter of some discussion in chess circles. I was a rising star and the chess-playing world had begun thinking of me as a mystery. From an obscure little town, with no family background in chess, with no famed master by my side, I had become a top-rated player. Between my own world rank and Kulikov's, there were only two players. I was certain that it was just a matter of time before I faced him in the world championships. The face off was inevitable. Chess was no longer a game or a sport for me even about winning cups and championships. It was a personal war against my nemesis, Andrei Kulikov.

Every time the press lauded me for my unique style of play, how I itched to tell them that it was Master who had got me this far. How I wished I could shout from the rooftop that Nandan Nath Upadhyaya was my master. The man who had gone beyond chess and its nuances, who cared not for riches nor recognition.

Time had passed as if in a hurry to get me to my destination. The gangly, fourteen-year-old Vasu was replaced by a robust one. I was twenty-three now, still in pursuit of my dream. Varun had married the girl of his dreams and settled down and Mira already had two lovely daughters. Father was nearing retirement and Master looked more and more frail with each passing year. I had know him for almost a decade. He was eighty-one now. Yet, he was no less a shark on the board. And my Rea was pursuing her master's degree in fine arts.

'My parents say that I'm obsessed with painting,' she told me one day.

'That's a good thing, because Master says no success is possible without obsession.'

'I don't paint for success, Vasu,' she said. 'I paint because I don't know what else to do when I miss you terribly, which is all the time.'

I knew where this was going, so I changed the topic.

'The world championship qualifiers are coming up, and—'

'When will you ask me the question, Vasu?' she said, interrupting me. 'I have been waiting very long.'

'You mean, when's the 70 per cent season-end sale starting?'

'Vasu! I'm serious.'

'As soon as I win the world championship, Rea.'

My answer hung between us for a while.

It didn't take an oracle to know exactly what Rea was thinking. What if I didn't win? The truth is there was a more practical issue to consider. I wasn't making enough money to pay even my own bills. How was I going to ensure that we were comfortable and had a secure future ahead of us? How would we go out for a dinner or a vacation if I was always worried about how much I had left in my account? I was still living on second-hand stuff. I had just inherited Varun's old motorcycle when he bought a new car. I still did not have an air-conditioner or air cooler in the scorching heat or sultry monsoons of north India. But I knew my time would come. Everything now rested on qualifying for the world championship and then winning it eventually.

'What are you giving your father on his retirement?' Rea asked, changing the topic.

'I won't be at the party.'

'Tell me you are joking!'

'No, Rea. I've to play the world championship qualifier so I can meet Andrei Kulikov.'

Rea felt that my father's retirement party was far more important. There would be many chances to play tournaments, but father would retire only once in his life. Perhaps she was right. But Andrei Kulikov had dwarfed everything else – maybe everyone else – for me.

Being the defending world champion, Kulikov didn't need to appear for the qualifiers, of course. He was the emperor and I was just an aspiring conqueror.

More than fifty GMs had participated in the world championship qualifiers. I knew I was going to win it right from the outset, though. Because I had to. For Master, for Rea. And I did. I coursed through that tournament like a stone going through water – unrestrained and unstoppable. I did not lose a single game.

It did not mean that things got any easier. It only meant there was only one thing between Andrei and me.

Time. Seven months.

A twenty-match world championship.

I managed to board an earlier flight after the qualifiers and reached home early. I had learnt to keep things quiet like my master and thought I would give everyone a surprise. Unfortunately, they had already heard on TV that Vasu Bhatt from India had qualified for the world championship. An Indian had made it to the championships after a gap of more than six decades.

Parked outside our house was a familiar vehicle. I knew I had seen it but couldn't recall whom it belonged to. I quietly opened the door and walked in to an unexpected scene. My parents were sitting in the guest room. Duggal uncle was having tea. Lying next to a plate of cookies was a pouch-like small bag and two bundles of cash.

Mira is already married, Varun too. Surely, father, who watches every penny, won't fork out so much money to buy jewellery. He doesn't even have two bundles of cash.

'What's going on?' I said. 'Namaste, uncle.'

'Vasu!' Mother hugged me joyfully. 'I heard on TV!'

Father quickly cleared the table. He stuffed the pouch into his pocket and handed the cash to Duggal uncle, who seemed taken aback by the sudden rush. Father shook his hand nervously to apprise our guest that I wasn't privy to what was going on.

'We missed you at the retirement party,' father said.

'What's going on, dad?'

'Have something to eat, Vasu,' mother interjected. 'You must be tired.'

'First tell me what's going on. What have we bought?'

'I'll take your leave, Bhattji,' Duggal uncle said and quickly got up. Adjusting the bulging bundles in his pockets, he walked out quickly.

'There's nothing to tell you, Vasu,' father said.

'First, let's eat something,' mother said in a hurry.

'Oh, for God's sake!' I shouted. 'Just tell me what both of you are up to.'

I reached out to my father's pocket to grab the pouch, but he pushed my hand away.

'Vasu!' he said. 'It's all sorted now.'

'What's sorted?'

They wouldn't answer.

'That's it,' I said, sitting down on the floor like I used to when I was a child. 'I won't eat or drink or get up from here till you tell me what's going on.'

'That's ridiculous, Vasu!' father prodded. 'Get up.'

'I swear I'm not budging till you tell me.'

He heaved a sigh.

'We just got your mother's jewellery back,' father said. 'We'd pawned it five years ago when we had to send you for Linares and other tournaments. I just got my provident fund money, so I used some of that to pay the remaining amount.'

I sat there, stunned. How come I hadn't noticed how plain mother had looked at Varun's wedding? Was I really so self-obsessed, so lost and engrossed in my own dreams? I had completely failed to see how, other than her mangalsutra and a nose pin, mother hadn't worn any jewellery for the past five years. I felt dizzy. And now, my father had spent his lifetime's savings – his provident fund – to get back something that should have never been given away in the first place. In five years, they must have returned at least double the amount. I felt like I had been kicked in the stomach.

How they had shielded me, protected me, put up with me all these years! And what did I give them in return?

'Why didn't you tell me?' I said. 'I had my winnings saved up from the last few tournaments. I could have chipped in.'

'Vasu,' mother said, 'don't we know how much books, travel and tournaments cost?'

'Besides,' father added, 'parents earn for their children, Vasu.'

'But you spent your lifetime's savings on me!' I felt like crying, washing their feet with my tears. All this while, so much had been going on right under my nose. But I had been too busy rushing in and out of the house for one tournament or the other, too busy to notice how they had been watching every penny. The GM title had come at the cost of their sacrifices.

In the last five years, I had come to believe that the new Vasu was different from the Vasu who had lost at Linares. But nothing had really changed. My parents had continued making sacrifices while I had been consumed by my need to excel. I was the same selfish Vasu, only older and much more confident, with a GM title to my name. Tears rolled down the corner of my eyes.

I turned my face away, but father turned me around by the shoulders and hugged me tight. I could hear his heartbeat. His body was not as stout as it used to be when I was a child, as if telling me that it no longer possessed the strength it once had. Over nine years had passed since I last hugged him. The last time was when he had allowed me to pursue chess with my master.

In the last nine years, I had hugged Rea countless times, but not my own father. The man who silently put up with all my nonsense, the one person who provided for me – how come I had never told him how much I loved him?

The humiliation of losing to Andrei Kulikov hadn't hit me as hard as the realization of my utter selfishness did now. No matter how many tournaments I won, I could not give them back the years that my selfishness had stolen away from them.

Seven months was all I had now to make them proud. The one thing for which they had toiled so hard was to make my dream come true. I realized in that split second that my dream was their dream too. Theirs and my master's.

14

KNITTING WITH ANDREI

THE DATE FOR the first match was set. 1/9/1992. Twenty games to be played over the next thirty days. I felt like an athlete preparing for years to give his everything in that nine-second run at the Olympics racetrack. It wasn't a you-win-some-you-lose-some situation; it was more like a you-win-now-or-you-will-be-eternally-forgotten situation. Everything I had worked for in the last nine years was at stake over the next thirty days.

With a minimum score of seven, whoever led with three points would be the world champion. Or whoever was ahead even by a point at the end of game twenty would be declared the winner, whichever occurred first. If the defending champion, Kulikov, and I, the challenger, ended up on equal points, he would retain the title.

One point for a win, half point for a draw and zero for a loss.

I was determined that my wins would be more than my losses at the end of thirty days. Then again, Andrei too would have his heart and mind set on winning. Besides, in the battle of minds, in a game like chess, my determination didn't mean much at the end of the day. I had no illusions about how towering was my goal, how lofty my dream.

The organizers had checked me into the Ritz Carlton at Battery Park in New York City, which was walking distance from the venue. It was by far the plushest hotel I had ever checked into. A private cab would pick me up at 4.30 p.m. every evening so I could be at the venue well in time. The game would start at 5 p.m. every day and could easily stretch past midnight.

'Bless me so I may win, Master,' I said over the phone.

'Go for a draw, Vasu,' he replied.

'Draw?'

'Andrei is an aggressive bull, Vasu,' he said, 'and draws will rattle him. Wait till he loses his patience.'

'What about the theoretical novelties we had coined?'

'No surprises early on. He'll up his game by several notches then. We go all out in the last eight games. Remember, Vasu,' he added, 'your patience will break Andrei more than your moves will.' A pause, then he concluded: 'Don't be the eager pawn. Be the graceful emperor.'

The venue was an ultra-quiet room on the 107th floor of the South Tower of World Trade Centre in Downtown Manhattan. It almost felt like I was up in the sky. If not for the absence of engine noise or the opulent living space, I might even have forgotten that I was not looking down at the tiny figurines and cars from an airplane but from a room. Numerous skyscrapers were visible, some more lit than others. Most of them had skeleton lighting on. Every now and then, you could see an ambulance or a police car zipping through the streets. You could only see the flashing beacons and never hear a siren from that height. In any case, the room was soundproof.

The carpet was plush and cushiony, the glass windows stretched from floor to ceiling. There were two attached washrooms, two couches, two chairs and a table. There was a little red button on the table to call the referee when needed. Two nameplates, our country flags, chess sheets with pencils and a chess clock rested on that table. Plus, there was the chessboard, of course. A live broadcast would televise the event throughout the world. Having said that, there isn't much to watch live in a chess game. But I suppose if we have fishing enthusiasts who patiently sit and wait for hours before the rod feels heavy, it's no surprise we have chess evangelists who want to see the game unfold before their very eyes.

The boardroom of a multi-billion-dollar financial institution had been provided for the world championship match. This was where a human (that was me) and a robot would compete. Really, he should have been named Android, for he looked more robot than a human to me. His hair slicked back from his forehead gave him a Nordic look. His charcoal-grey suit was fitted to perfection, tailored to his slim physique.

Of course, I didn't lose sight of the fact that behind this well-groomed look was an eccentric chess player of extraordinary calibre, someone who couldn't care less about what he wore.

The old Andrei Kulikov was known to play in tees and jeans, and to show up for the most important games with an unshaven face and ruffled hair. His sponsor, a large software company, had nearly gone to court, forcing Andrei to dress formally.

Other than that, nothing had changed about him in the last four years except his rating and ranking, both of which had gone up significantly. A world No. 1, the current world champion, with the highest-ever ELO rating of 2920; the only giveaway that he was not an alien or a robot chiselled to perfection were his fingernails. Despite the well-manicured hand his finger nails seemed to be embedded deep into the skin. Oh well, maybe he had bitten more than he could chew.

His lack of courtesy was as consistent as his play had been over the years. Once again, during the first match, he extended a limp hand without looking at me. I felt as if I were holding a thawed piece of chicken leg.

He might be the current world champion, but I didn't get here twiddling my thumbs over a chessboard either. Kulikov's coldness gave me a strange strength this time. I found it more amusing than intimidating. He seemed like a stunned automaton, as inanimate as any pawn on the board. I wondered if he remembered me from Linares.

Kulikov was to open with white.

'Ready?' The referee said and, starting the clock, walked away into the next room. There would be no one else in the room other than Kulikov and I.

Kulikov made his move before the referee even stepped out of our room. A standard king's pawn opening.

For a moment, my heart fluttered, stomach churned and the hair on my hands stood on end. This was the world championship. Against Andrei Kulikov. Out of hundreds and thousands of players in the world, I alone had made it here. This was the tournament after which you would either be the beloved world champion or the famous loser. I shook off all thoughts and looked at the chessboard, and just like that my mind was yoked to it.

Everything went by the book for the first twenty moves and then my robot friend offered an exchange of knights. If I didn't go for the exchange, he could take my bishop for his knight, gaining a slight material advantage. And if I opted for the exchange, my knight in play would be gone, giving him a space advantage – more room to play. Yet, the exchange would benefit me because he would end up with doubled pawns on e-file, an important centre column. This was unusual because, clearly, doubled pawns or two pawns on the same file create a weakness. No GM, especially a world champion, could make that dumb a move. Surely he couldn't possibly think that I would let him take my bishop. Unlike the queen move at Linares, this was not something he could take back. Where was the trap? Why did he throw me this bait? Why would he weaken his position? What was he thinking? I thought hard. For thirty minutes, without blinking. I couldn't believe he had made that error.

I went for the exchange and looked him in the eye. He should know I had picked up on his mistake.

Kulikov made the next five moves at lightning speed, as if he were playing rapid chess at the local club and not a world championship match. He had it all worked out. The gravity of my own mistake only hit me a little later when I was down by a pawn with an exposed centre seized by his bishops. Then, he castled on the queen side, which was now an impregnable fortress with a three-base pawn chain, and went all out to mate my king.

The game wrapped up on the forty-eighth move. I resigned before he announced checkmate.

The result?

Andrei Kulikov: 1. Vasu Bhatt: 0.

'Master, he knocked my socks off!' I called and reported the result.

'Calm down, Vasu. Walk me through your moves.'

We both set up chessboards at our end.

As soon as we got to the twentieth move and Master heard me take that knight, he exclaimed, 'That's a blunder, son!'

'But his pawns would be doubled!' I brought his attention to this important point.

He continued without asking me about my next move, 'Doubling of pawns is a small price to pay here for opening the f-file for attack. He'll line up his bishops on b2 and c3, then castle his king on the queen-side, double his rooks on f, and end up with a strong pawn chain which he'll soon open to attack your weak f7 and h7. This will force you to give up a pawn and retreat your minor pieces. You'll lose on tempo and material. Another nine moves, and your queen will be cornered protecting the king, while his would be dancing behind his rooks.'

'That's exactly what he did, Master!'

'Listen, Vasu,' he said, 'don't forget, even for a moment, that you are playing the world championship. Don't go for easy victories and draws. You can only beat him with caution and patience. When anything looks too good to be true, it probably is.'

'Should I go for one of our novelties tomorrow?'

'No. Stick to our plan. Don't worry. He'll come around. He'll err. Every human does.'

'Do you think I still have a chance?'

'Vasu!' he chuckled. 'We've only just started. No one's invincible. We'll leave him gasping for breath from Game 13.'

Master patiently went through the rest of the game, identifying areas where I could have salvaged the situation. It was a long phone call.

I wrote down whatever I could recall from our conversation and pasted it on the mirror in my washroom. I spent the next few hours playing practice games.

The next day, and at every subsequent game, I extended a flaccid hand too. We were merely touching hands to complete the formality of a handshake. That automaton though, showed no reaction at my change of demeanour. This went on for the next eight games that were drawn without any major drama. At the end of nine games, the score was 5–4.

We were getting used to each other. I was even beginning to develop a slight affinity with him. I would jump out of bed each morning with Andrei's cold fish of a face flashing in front of my eyes and eagerly go through practice throughout the day to meet him, to mate him in the evening.

I would always call Master before leaving for my games and, in every phone call, he would remind me to be extremely patient and go for closed games that are clogged in the centre and require mind-numbing tactical play.

'Shouldn't I take more risks?' I asked.

'Wait and watch, Vasu, he'll make a blunder. He will.'

'But he doesn't show any reaction at all! He has no fear.'

Master laughed. 'He may not show it, but he does have fear. Everyone does. Fear of loss. And we'll exploit it at the right time.'

GAME 10.
Score at the end of the game. Andrei: 5; Vasu: 5.

Exactly as Master had predicted, Andrei faltered. I couldn't be sure if he had gone for a reckless line of variation because of impatience, complacency or overconfidence, but whatever it was, I registered my first victory against the current world champion, Andrei Kulikov.

And the wonder of all wonders, my master had been by my side all this while. Every time I needed to speak to him on the phone, he was available. It was a double victory.

'Master!' I screamed over the phone. 'I won! I won!'

'Vasu,' he said plainly, 'we have to be ultra-careful now. He'll come back with a vengeance. He's going to up the stakes. Play by the book.'

Game 11.

I opened with white and played exactly as Master had told me. The result was a predictable draw.

The scoreboard read: Andrei: 5.5; Vasu: 5.5.

Game 12.

Today, the chess robot walked into the room more like a human. His eyes were a bit red, as if he had been up all night. He wasn't walking like Michael Jackson taking the centre stage, but more like a Rottweiler herding sheep – with a certain uncertainty. What really gave away his change in temperament, though, was the way he shook hands. His grip was firm. I kept mine limp. For the first time in fifteen days, he looked me in the eye.

To my surprise, although not completely, Kulikov chose an aggressive and risky opening. Sicilian Dragon. In the past fifty years, no GM had played this opening in any tournament, let alone in a world championship. There was very little research material on it. I didn't know many lines of variations on this. I would have loved to play by the book, but the truth was, books had very little to say about this opening. I didn't think anyone in their sane mind would even consider the Sicilian Dragon. One tiny miscalculation on either side would be enough to lose a point.

The risky opening paid off for Andrei. He smothered me in thirty-two moves. Today was the first time that I understood why he was called the chess missile. It was a clinical attack of ruthless precision. Yet, I was okay. Not afraid or down. I was still itching to show him what I had up my sleeves. If not for Master's instructions to play safe for the first twelve games, I would have gone for it already. All things aside, the score stood at 6.5–5.5.

I called Master from my room, but he didn't pick up the phone. I dialled a second time, but there was no reply. I didn't

get mad. After all, Master was an old man. He was probably in
the washroom, or had stepped out to get veggies from the street
vendor. Besides, it wasn't like I had any exciting news to report.

I waited for about fifteen minutes and called again. No reply.
I called yet again, another fifteen minutes later. No reply again.
This was a bit worrying. It was nearly midnight in New York and
I wanted to catch up on my sleep, but I didn't want to hit the
sack without speaking to Master.

While waiting for his call, I picked up the day's sheet to see
how I could have handled the game differently. At least ten
possibilities emerged immediately upon a brief examination. I
could have chosen better replies to Sicilian Dragon. A couple of
hours passed as I examined multiple lines of variations. I could
have easily parried his attack. The phone rang.

'Vasu?' It was father. 'Hope I didn't wake you up.'

It was a pleasant surprise to hear my father's voice. He rarely
called me when I was away on tournaments.

'I was trying to reach Master, in fact,' I said. 'How's everyone?'

'He had to urgently leave for his village.'

My heart jumped to my mouth but I knew that the cause
must have been absolutely pressing and unavoidable. This was
the one thing he had been preparing me for the last nine years.

'He told me to pass on this message to you: Follow the plan.
No deviations.'

Father seemed somewhat uncomfortable speaking more
on the phone as he hung up almost immediately. He must be
concerned about my sleep time, I thought.

Game 13 and 14. Master's strategy worked flawlessly.

Andrei opened with Queen's Gambit in Game 13 but I
declined and went for Semi Slav, quickly shifting to the more
unusual Chigorian variation. This took Andrei utterly by surprise.

I remember how he gulped down a whole cup of coffee as if it were a tequila shot. I continued to build a tight centre because, more than going for a straight win, my goal was to frustrate him. Out of that frustration would sprout a mistake that would lead me to build a winning attack. Master had trained me in all major lines of variations on Queen's Gambit and Gambit Declined.

All this while, I had played closed and tight games, avoiding exchanging pieces, keeping the centre locked, dragging on with the extra time. And, exactly as Master had said it would, this had given Kulikov an impression of what sort of player I was. He had mistaken my portrayed patience and tactical play as my inherent chess temperament. The truth was, I had always been an impatient, angry and aggressive player. Something I had managed to hide in the championship so far.

In Game 14, I went all out with an opening that shook Andrei. He was forced to drop his hide.

Playing with white, I went for Vienna Game, a semi-aggressive opening. Giving the illusion of a playable opening, I offered a delayed King's Gambit. This made Andrei think hard and long. He used over twenty-five minutes on this move. But that was only the beginning. Nandan Nath Upadhyaya had prepared me to turn this tender jolt into a catastrophic earthquake. Just when he was settling in, I went for the Frankenstein–Dracula variation. The rest, as they say, is history.

It had been quite something to watch Andrei drink coffee like there was no tomorrow. His digestive tract had processed more than fifty cups in the last two days. Like a boiled egg, each tap was cracking him. The human side – soft and shaky – of the chess automaton was emerging.

The score on 20 September 1992 after fourteen games – Andrei: 6.5; Vasu: 7.5.

Games 15, 16, 17 and 18 resulted in draws. That the last four games ended in draws was not as interesting a fact as how they had ended in draws. All four games had drawn on a mutual-draw offer, with Kulikov offering to draw in three of the four games. Maybe he had saved up some nasty surprises for the last two games. He needed to win only one game to retain his title.

End of Game 18 – Andrei: 8.5; Vasu: 9.5.

Everything was going as planned in the tournament, except that Master was still not back from his village and he hadn't called me all this while. But this time I wasn't angry at all, for I knew that if there was anyone who lived selflessly in this world, it was my master.

I was concerned about his health, but since father said that he had only gone to his village, I took heart.

27 September was a free day and my mind was tired from the endless grilling of the past many days. I thought of taking a break to freshen up my mind. There was nothing else to prepare. I knew my responses to any opening Andrei might choose. I popped a pill so I could sleep through the day. I had a light dinner and took another pill to get some good sleep. On the morning of the twenty-eighth, I casually picked up the *New York Times* over breakfast.

It carried an article by Olga Pyzik, the second ex-wife of the thirty-eight-year-old Andrei Kulikov. She was in New York to launch her book *My Years with Andrei*. The article cited the following passage from the book.

Saving a few times, like when he was sleeping, living with Andrei was a continuous challenge. He was just not designed with any sense of living in a world sans chess. He couldn't even pour tea without spilling it in the saucer. He would never remember to turn the gas off after cooking. And the only thing he knew how to cook was an omelette. It was scary to be in the same car with him because he would just stop anywhere and start making notes on some game.

He would forget his wallet in the restaurant and keys in his car. It's hard to imagine that the genius Andrei, immaculate on the chessboard, would be so clumsy in real life. The man who could think through lengthy lines of variations in his head could not string together two words to hold a conversation. He never spoke to my parents. He would say he didn't have any conversational skills. Surely, he could have learnt these skills, if only he had made an effort.

I kept my hopes up for six long years and then one day I realized that 'if only' doesn't work with people like Andrei. If it could, he wouldn't be Andrei then.

I wondered if I was destined to read that article today, for as soon as I put the paper aside, something inside me changed. I no longer thought of him as a pretentious snob, but a man who was just wired that way. A wave of sympathy washed over my hard feelings for Kulikov, no, Andrei. I had known him for days now. But sympathy has no place in chess. There is room for variations, for mistakes, for a whole range of human emotions but not sympathy. You show sympathy and you are dead. If you spare your lunch, your opponent will have you for lunch.

I thought of Andrei's misdemeanours, his sarcastic advice to me so I could once again feel a surge of anger towards him. As Master had said, my anger was my energy and at Game 19 of the World Championship, I couldn't afford to lose even a tiny fraction of an ounce.

Game 19. When Andrei walked in, the article I'd read that morning kept flashing in front of me. I couldn't help but offer a firm grip for the customary handshake. I felt that I had been judging him, and I had no right to. But all my feelings took a backseat when, once again, like the first time, he made no attempt to shake hands. Any emotion or feeling of sympathy quickly left me, but it took my mental peace along. I felt agitated and angry.

Things didn't get any better when Andrei absolutely shocked me with the most aggressive display of his game. Maybe he had read the article too. He practically rammed into me and, from the sixth move onwards, I was on the defence. It was a humiliating defeat with his mating attack materializing on the twenty-eighth move.

He pushed his pawn, checking my king, and turned it 360 degrees in the square as if he were screwing it in.

'Checkmate,' he announced. There was elation in his voice. And that smirk. The I-told-you-to-take-up-knitting-instead smirk was most humiliating. I felt like breaking the glass and jumping from the 107th floor and landing on some yellow cab parked underneath. This image wasn't too far off from the reality because, figuratively speaking, my final position on the board today had been something like that.

Score at the end of Game 19 – Andrei: 9.5; Vasu: 9.5.

I walked back to my room greatly distressed. The game progressed so fast that I didn't even know what the hell actually happened. Why did I change my tempo? Why did I lose my patience? I couldn't forgive myself. I missed Master terribly. I wished I knew his village contact number. I wished he would call me.

The chances of winning the final game were very slim because Andrei would play by the book. To retain the title, he didn't have to win. He just had to draw. If I lost the last game, I would lose; and I would lose even if I drew it. He wouldn't take any chances. He didn't need to.

I called Master's home, out of sheer desperation. I called father to find out if he had made any contact. No luck. I sat there thinking about what I could possibly play next against Andrei in my last game.

Master, Master, where are you? I prayed with all my strength.

A soft voice spoke in my head. 'What would Master do if he were playing?'

Of course. Master is here, with you, right now. Your master is in the training he's given you all these years, Vasu.

I knew what to do.

I spent the whole of the next day going through old games of unconventional openings. That's what Master would do. He would surprise Andrei. He would choose an opening where it would just not be possible for Andrei to play by the book.

Game 20. I tried to reach Master again in the morning, but no luck. Somewhere in the deepest corner of my heart, the corner reserved for my dreams, I kind of accepted that I might not win the World Championship. That I might not be able to make my folks proud this time around. *But I will come back for you, Andrei Kulikov.* By that I did not mean that I had given up. I had every intention to fight till the last pawn stood on the board.

I walked in right when the game was about to start. Casually, while I was sitting down, I extended my hand without looking at Andrei. The referee pressed the button and the clock began ticking.

Playing with white, I went for an opening no one in their right mind would pick. Not against Andrei anyway. But I did. Because that's what Master would do. I went for Grob's Attack – one of the least played and least respected openings. The chances of a draw were next to nil with this one. I would either win or lose. I knew instantly that it startled him; he raised his eyes and settled his gaze on mine for a few seconds right after I opened.

Andrei thought for over ten minutes before responding to my first move. Ten minutes. No GM invests ten minutes on the opening move. Three moves later, I went in for the variation – Keene Defence. Andrei thought for another fifteen minutes. Meanwhile, he had already downed two cups of coffee. Double-shot espressos.

He was cautious as expected and I was reckless, which perhaps was also expected. Like when you throw a stray dog a morsel with the intention of kicking it when it approached you, Andrei offered me a gambit. He was happy to lose a pawn to gain mobility of pieces. Rather than taking his gambit, I went for another line of variation, even more dangerous, the Romford Countergambit. Andrei drank three cups of coffee before making his next move. I was thirty minutes ahead in time advantage. But thirty minutes mean nothing if you have no attack or defence. I had the chance to build my attack.

At move seventeen came my first breakthrough when I got the opportunity to plant my knight on g6, safely nested in his V-pawn chain, protected by my pawn on h5. My king was safely castled on the queen side. But it wasn't till the twenty-third move, when my rooks aligned to launch a catastrophe on the g-file behind my knight, that the mighty Andrei Kulikov got up and began pacing up and down the room.

He was mumbling to himself, shaking his right hand in the air. He sat on the couch and threw his head back, but got up the very next moment and resumed pacing up and down. He got back on the table and pressed the red button for more coffee. He gulped one cup and another. Five in a row. Got up to go to the washroom. He opened the door of the washroom and rather than entering, he rushed back to the table. Andrei kept staring at the board and then went up and down the room again.

Finally, he advanced his pawn on the b-file. It wouldn't take a GM to know that his position was hopeless on the king side, where my offence was going strong. The only way out for him was to launch a counter-attack on the queen side, where my king was castled. But it was a little too late for that. My other knight jumped to the king side attack in two hops and with my bishops already lined, I went into his fort like I had nothing to lose.

One sacrifice of a bishop and another three moves later, his king stood there, fully exposed. He was officially screwed.

Andrei got up began pacing up and down the room again. He sat on the couch and had some more coffee. I had lost count of how many by now. I could smell victory. I was barely three moves away. All forced moves, where Andrei had no choice.

We were only twenty-nine moves into the game and I could see my master smiling. He appeared in the soft lighting of the room like a guardian angel, smiling at me. I felt that he was saying to me, 'I'm proud of you, son. I knew you had it in you. I knew it.' His eyes seemed moist. Mine were too.

Andrei returned to the table and looked at me. His mask was still impenetrable, but his eyes held a sort of admiration. Something like the spark that lit up my eyes when I had asked the GMs for autographs during my first rated tournament in Bangalore.

He got up again and went to the washroom. I was somewhat worried when he didn't emerge for almost ten minutes. I nearly called the referee, but he came back and sat at the table. He stared at me again, with the look that an avid chess player would have in the middle of an epiphany, as if he had chanced upon a winning attack. For a moment, my heart pounded and

I looked at the board again. Had I made a mistake? Andrei looked so assured.

His hand hovered over his side of the board and eventually landed on his king. I was a bit surprised because it was not in check and, with the pawns in front gone, there was no sense in moving the king.

He lifted his king by its crown and laid it gently on the board.

'I resign,' he said and extended his arm to shake hands. Andrei Kulikov shaking hands at the finish.

'I knit all right, don't I?' I said, gripping his hand a little longer than needed.

'Excuse me?' he said, a little puzzled.

I just looked at the scoreboard that read Andrei: 9.5; Vasu: 10.5.

It was time to go down for the press conference.

15

MOVE YOUR FOOT SOLIDER

A NDREI FADED AWAY into the background as I walked through the corridors, stepping on a plush carpet to catch up with our referee and two executives in impeccable suits. They had been sent to escort the new world chess champion to the podium, I figured. I couldn't help but cast one last glance in Andrei's direction; my opponent stood looking outside the big glass window.

You did it, Vasu! World Chess Champion!

I braced myself for the media frenzy and the autographs that would follow the win. I even racked my brain for a suitable response to 'how do you feel about being the new world champion?' I certainly didn't want to flounder and fumble like a bumbling idiot on an international broadcast after winning the No. 1 title.

To my surprise, there were no journalists waiting with bated breath to get a quote from me, no mics or flashing cameras either. For a fraction of a second I was disappointed to see the silent boardroom. There were four people in expensive business suits seated around a long table. The very air reeked of power and wealth. One of the more friendly faces of the four got up. He was at once tall and imposing.

'Congratulations, Mr Bhatt,' he said, shaking a firm hand. 'I'm Anatoly Zaslavsky. The A-Z of Chess.' Everyone joined him in the laughter.

Anatoly Zaslavsky was the chairman of FIDE, and I wasn't expecting to meet him right away. Then again, I didn't really know what all came with victory. He introduced me to other people in the room who were executives of a Fortune 500 company.

'Mr Murphy James is the CEO of GEM, Global Enterprise Machines,' Anatoly said. 'They are the platinum sponsor of this tournament and have something for you here.'

'We've been watching you grow over the last few years, Mr Bhatt,' Murphy said. 'We would like to offer you a five-year, $2 million exclusive sponsorship deal. In particular, to endorse our range of supercomputers. We are entering in the Indian market in a big way.'

I didn't know whether to jump in the air and touch the ceiling or appear solemn and serious like them, pretending that it was a routine matter.

Instantly, my mother's face flashed before me. My mother, who had pawned her jewellery and lived without it for four years; my father, who had emptied his provident fund to pay for my expenses. Master's old clothes, his bicycle, our basic no-frills home, old motorcycle … it all came to my mind. How easily I could enrich their lives. Another man, whom Murphy introduced as Richard Cook, their legal counsel, smiled at me and gently slid a one-page document in front of me. A Mont Blanc pen was resting on it.

'We will send the detailed contract to your attorney,' Richard said. 'You can sign your conditional consent here. This simply means that, unless you find something unacceptable in our contract, you will not back out. Plus, we'll have the first right of refusal if you go with any other sponsor.'

I picked up the pen to seize the golden opportunity, but a voice inside stopped me.

Can you say, Vasu, that this victory belongs to you and you alone?

'I'm sorry, gentlemen.' I put the pen down. 'I can't sign without the consent of my master.'

'Your master?' Anatoly exclaimed. 'I don't recall you making a mention of him at any of the events before.'

'All in good time, Mr Zaslavsky,' I said, feeling a sense of pride for Master.

After a few whispers amongst themselves, they upped the offer by another $5,00,000. They wanted to announce the deal at the press conference, they told me. So there *was* a press conference. Good. When I declined again, they handed me their business cards and said they would wait. We were led to the media room by Zaslavsky who flung open the door dramatically, his hands pointing in my direction, and declared, 'Here, I give you the new chess world champion!'

The media room was packed with journalists, dignitaries and various notables. I was bathed in the flashlights of shutterbugs.

Wow! All these people are here for me!

I felt overwhelmed, underprepared. Smiling, I opened the bottle of water and took a sip in style. Calling me a chess protégé, an original thinking machine from India, Zaslavsky gave a long statement. He said my style of play reminded him of some of the greatest chess players of all time. I tried my best to not let my expressions betray my feelings. Within, I was bursting with joy and pride, but on the outside, I maintained a steady, even artificial smile.

It was an exhilarating experience to be recognized on the

world stage for all the sacrifices everyone in my life and I had made. I wished they were there with me. I was handed the World Cup, a gleaming, shiny beauty I could see my own reflection in. I gripped it tightly and planted a kiss on it. I never told this to Rea, but kissing the cup was a feeling like no other. US $10,00,000 – that was my prize money. It was fifty times more than the first prize I'd won at the last international tournament.

'How does it feel to be the next world champion?' a journalist asked me.

This was a question I had dreamed of being asked for nine long years. All the fun I had missed out on, the effort I put in, all the defeats I faced, struggles I went through – the sole objective of it all was that one day I would be on stage, with many people peeking through their cameras, some holding voice recorders in their hands, some taking notes, when someone would get up, point his pen at me and ask me this question.

I cleared my throat.

'Imagine that you spend years and years of your life digging a tunnel. While eating, sleeping, bathing, resting, working, that's all you think about – your tunnel. That's all you work on. Your tunnel becomes your life. Your friends, peers and others keep excelling in life, they continue to flourish and progress, while you are chiselling away, one blow at a time, stuck in that tunnel. Your friends move into new houses and buy bigger cars, while you continue to pinch pennies.

'You remain soiled, hungry, lacking, even poor, but you don't give up because you believe in your dream. You only have hope that one day you'll see the other end of this tunnel, but you can't be sure. You cry, you laugh, you struggle, resist, battle, you feel depressed at times, but you keep pushing, and pushing, and then one day your blow has a different sound. It's not as full, you feel just a thin layer separating you from the outside. Your heart throbs in anticipation. You hit harder and the hammerhead goes through.

'And then, light stares at you. Right in your eyes. The light you have been waiting for. A gust of fragrant wind from outside cools your sweaty brows. You take a deep breath and you smell victory. It feels unreal, unbelievable, incredible. You pinch yourself to make sure you aren't dreaming. And, for once, your reality is better than your wildest dreams. That's how I feel right now.'

There was loud applause after a long spell of silence. It was overwhelming to see so many strangers rejoice at my success.

'We noticed that your style of play in the last eight games was markedly different from anything you have ever played till date,' a veteran chess reporter said. 'What would you say about that?'

'It was the plan. My master taught me four unconventional openings with many lines of defence exclusively for this tournament—'

'We've never heard about your coach before!' a senior female reporter from the *New York Times* said, cutting in. 'What's his name?'

I went quiet. The world should know that my master is not just anybody but the greatest genius ever known to the chess world. Many seconds ticked by and I kept quiet. Almost for a minute.

'Mr Bhatt, what's hi—'

'Nandan Nath Upadhyaya.' I leaned forward and spoke softly into the mike.

Suddenly, the room was abuzz with whispers and chatter.

The FIDE chairman got up from his seat and looked at me.

'*The* Nandan Nath Upadhyaya? Of 1938 fame?' he said.

'Yes. The one and only.'

A slip was pushed out to me by Richard Cook, which read: 'US$50,00,000. Our final offer.'

'Is he here, your master?' another one said. 'Can he come on the stage?'

'He's a bit of a recluse. That would be an understatement, actually.' I chuckled.

'We heard GEM has signed an exclusive sponsorship deal with you,' a reporter said. 'Would you like to share the details?'

I looked at Murphy James and Richard Cook and smiled.

'We are in advanced negotiations at this stage,' I said, adding jokingly, 'they are offering me more than I can handle.'

'Mr Bhatt,' a young reporter asked, 'when did you take up chess?'

'After I failed in grade two in school.'

The whole house roared with laughter.

For the next one hour, they asked me all sorts of questions, ranging from how I met my master to how eating broccoli helped chess players perform better.

I went straight to my room and called home. I couldn't wait to hear their excited voices. They already knew. Varun told me over the phone that a pack of reporters from leading dailies had reached my home and were currently sitting in my living room, having chai-pakora while interviewing my parents and quizzing them about the whereabouts of Nandan Nath Upadhyaya.

Father said that Master had given him his contact details, and agreed that we would immediately leave for his village upon my arrival. I felt relieved and light beyond words. Many bad thoughts had crossed my mind. Thank God there was no truth to them. I was finally going to see my master and share our success.

I turned down all invitations for exhibition games and media interviews, and took the next flight to India. To see Nandan Nath Upadhyaya.

Many reporters were already waiting for me at Delhi airport. I answered a few questions briefly and, tearing through them, rushed to my taxi. It's only when I got closer to home that I realized that I hadn't bought any gifts for anyone. Master was all I had thought about.

I knew they would have made great preparations at home for a grand celebration, but I was in no mood to do anything without Master. Varun and Mira would be there. Rea would be waiting too. But what fun would it be without Master? He didn't even know how his Vasu had played the last game to win the championship. The thing on top of my priority list was to see his reaction when I showed him how I trampled Andrei Kulikov. What would he say when I told him about the exclusive sponsorship offer? I hoped, wished and prayed that his impenetrable mask of indifference would slip off just this one time at least. The dream we had together, the dream he had dreamed with his wife had now been made real.

Mother came running outside as soon as my taxi reached home. She put some mustard oil at the entrance to protect me from the evil eye. Father joined her soon after along with Varun and Mira. A couple of reporters were waiting outside my home and they promptly took pictures. Varun managed to distract them as they approached me to ask questions.

'Master's not back yet, right?' I asked my father as soon as I set eyes on.

He just shook his head.

Mother had baked a small cake. Her smile and the cake had one thing in common – both looked down and beaten.

What's going on? Is this how we'll celebrate this victory? My World Championship?

'We'll leave for Master's village in the morning. Let's have dinner now,' mother said.

'Yes, Vasu,' father said. 'You must be tired and hungry.'

Varun seemed distant; Mira too. She had left her daughters behind with her husband. Something was amiss and I couldn't quite figure out what.

'Am I missing something?' I asked. 'You guys don't seem very happy at my victory.'

'No, Vasu,' mother came running and cupped my face. 'We are over the moon.'

'Of course, I just mean—'

'Let's have dinner first.'

I was quick to catch that subtle nuance.

'First? You mean there's something.'

'No, Vasu, there's—'

'There's something you should know, Vasu,' father intervened.

A hush fell over the place. Mother was shaking her head and looking at father, asking him to wait until later.

'Your master is no more.'

'No more?' I said collapsing into my chair. 'But I just won the championship for him!'

Father came close and held me by my shoulder, but I gently shrugged him off.

No more. Master was no more.

Never to return.

Nandan Nath Upadhyaya. Gone.

No tears trickled down. I didn't feel queasy nor sick.

'His body?'

'He was cremated in the hospital crematorium as per his will.'

'Hospital?'

'Master had been sick for many years, Vasu,' father said, pulling up a bit closer. 'He had lung cancer and had been admitted to hospital on numerous occasions. It seems every time he went to the village, he was actually in the hospital.'

That master strategist had it all worked out. I hated him. I should have known that the secretive genius would depart the way he had lived – quietly. He always had the last word anyway.

Why didn't he tell me? He could have! He should have!

'I must go to Master's home right away, father.'

'We can't, Vasu.'

'What do you mean we can't?' I almost shouted at him.

'He left the will with his lawyer, along with the house keys. It was his lawyer who informed us of his death.' He added that a meeting was already scheduled the following morning.

I walked into my room without another word. It was a still night. Like wet wood burns slowly, producing more smoke than heat, my heart was smouldering inside. I wished to see Master at least once. *Just* once. I wished I could share one cola with him, our last bubbly.

I opened my old chess notes where Master had scribbled many things in his scrawny handwriting. I stroked the letters as if they somehow allowed me to reach out and touch him. I looked at the phone in the room, wishing he would just call asking me how I fared in the championship. Or that he would just show up, gently ringing the bell and I would rush out to take his bicycle from him and park it properly. Or he would be kind enough to lash out at me for losing the penultimate game in the championship, or for not signing the big sponsorship deal. Who knew what he would do or how he would react.

There were two other people waiting at the lawyer's office in the morning. One of them was not unknown to us.

'This is Dr D'Souza, chief neurosurgeon and a trustee at St. John's hospital,' the lawyer said, 'and he is Mr Singh, chairman of the Department of Language and Arts, and a government-appointed trustee of St. John's hospital.'

I couldn't really see the connection. What were the trustees of a hospital doing here?

'There's a letter Mr Anand Sharma left for you.'

The lawyer gave me an envelope.

Finally, something from my master. My beloved master.

It was dated a week before his death.

My dear Vasu, my son,

When you read this letter, I'll be no more. I know you have won the championship. And what I also know is that 'Vasu, the World Champion' will mourn my loss for a long time. He'll regret the last bottle of cola that he couldn't share with his master to celebrate his victory.

Everyone has to die one day, Vasu. How one dies is immaterial. What's more important is how one lives. I'm at peace as I write to you, for I've made good on my promise to Uma.

Success holds in itself a unique spark that only a rare few have. I saw that spark in you nine years ago. I always knew you were destined to be a champion. It couldn't be any other way for my son.

Some stuff I'm leaving behind for you. Start a chess school.

I'm proud of you. Always have been.

Master

A tear trickled down my cheeks, which I quickly wiped away.

'Mr Anand Sharma has bequeathed all his assets – including 90 acres of land in his native village and his house – in your name, along with a responsibility,' the lawyer told me.

I was silent.

'Mr Bhatt,' he continued. 'Mr Sharma was the biggest donor and chief trustee of St. John's hospital. He has nominated you in his place. Mr Singh and Dr D'Souza are here to authorize your appointment.'

'We are honoured to have you aboard, Mr Bhatt,' they said. 'Mr Anand Sharma always spoke very highly of you.'

'Nandan Nath Upadhyaya.'

'Sorry?' they mumbled.

'Master was Nandan Nath Upadhyaya. World chess champion. Not Anand Sharma.'

They looked at me blankly, as if I were speaking in Mandarin. I must have looked a little crazed to them, but it didn't matter.

'Can I please have his house keys?'

The lawyer took my signature at a few places to complete the legal formalities. I told father that I wanted to go and spend a few hours at Master's on my own.

The hustle-bustle outside his home, in the street, was still the same, as if nothing had happened. Some children were playing cricket, a vegetable hawker was passing through, Bollywood songs were blaring loudly on someone's TV. A neighbour was dumping garbage from the first floor onto the street.

I stood outside Master's home. My hand automatically reached out to the doorbell. That had been my ritual for the last nine years. Master might just come out. I let a few minutes pass. I could feel my lower lip trembling. I unlocked the door and bolted it behind me. I collected the newspapers lying in the lobby from the last few days, took them inside, and flung them on the couch.

The house had a musty smell. Of a closed house, of Master's house, of Master. Like the blanket of night that covers the buzz of the day, a strange shroud of peace made me mushy inside.

I walked to the fridge and opened two bottles of cola. I put one next to his chair and one on my side. And then I waited because it felt like he would just emerge from the other room or the washroom and sit in his chair. I wished it were all just a set-up to surprise me. But no one came and sat down to enjoy his cola with me. I was mad at Master. I waited nine years to make him proud and he couldn't wait nine days.

As I sat on the floor, next to his rocking chair, tears began rolling down. Master liked everything in its place. The mess of newspapers I had just created was staring at me. I waited for Master to just chastise me for leaving them like that. But he didn't. I got up to organize and stack the newspapers, and a pamphlet fell out of one of them. It was an invitation to a local event for a token entry fee. It reminded me of Master even more.

I opened the cupboard in his bedroom. His clothes, old but clean, were hanging immaculately. I took my clothes off and put his on. Master was lean but I was leaner. His shirt was a little loose, but it didn't matter much as one of his sweaters fit me alright. It was a hand-knit sweater, neatly patched at two places. I took one of his mufflers and, wrapping it around my head and neck, pulled it slightly over my chin. I could feel his presence around me.

I saw myself in the mirror and a smile broke out on my face. With a stubble of two days and wearing Master's clothes, I looked like I could have been a relative, maybe even his son. I took out his bicycle, checked the air pressure and cleaned the seat with a tiny piece of cloth Master always hid just under the seat. Locking the door, I glanced at the address on the pamphlet and rode down to the venue. A school. It was the weekend, and many children had gathered around two chess players having a casual game during the tournament break. I quietly stood there, next to the talkative and eager kids.

Modern children, dressed nicely.

It was an interesting game. They leaned forward to study the chessboard closely.

'*Paidal chalao*,' I said.

The children burst into laughter. Tears welled up in my eyes, remembering every tiny detail of the morning I had met my master nine years ago.

I looked at their faces, searching for an impatient pair of eyes.

Eyes with a spark in them.

Made in the USA
Middletown, DE
03 April 2018